THE CASE OF THE MISSING DOLL

L A MORRALL

Copyright

Copyright © 2023 by L A Morrall

All rights reserved.

No portion of this book may be reproduced in any form without written permission from the publisher or author, except as permitted by U.S. copyright law.

About the Author

L.A. Morrall, a lifetime fan of film noir, resides in England's "Creative County" of Staffordshire.

W ORKING AS A PROFESSIONAL photographer by day, in his down time he loves to escape into the worlds of dark video games, and of course the classic film noir movies of the 1940s and 1950s he grew up watching on British TV (and those he is still discovering.) Stars such as Humphrey Bogart, Ida Lupino, Victor Mature and Gloria Grahame are among his favourites from this great artistic American movement of the 20th Century.

Beginning as a social media status on his birthday, and becoming a serialised story in weekly updates, L.A. Morrall was driven by the enthusiasm and support of Facebook friends to complete a story that seemed to almost write itself, as the characters and fictional city came to life before his very eyes.

In Memory of the great Ida Lupino

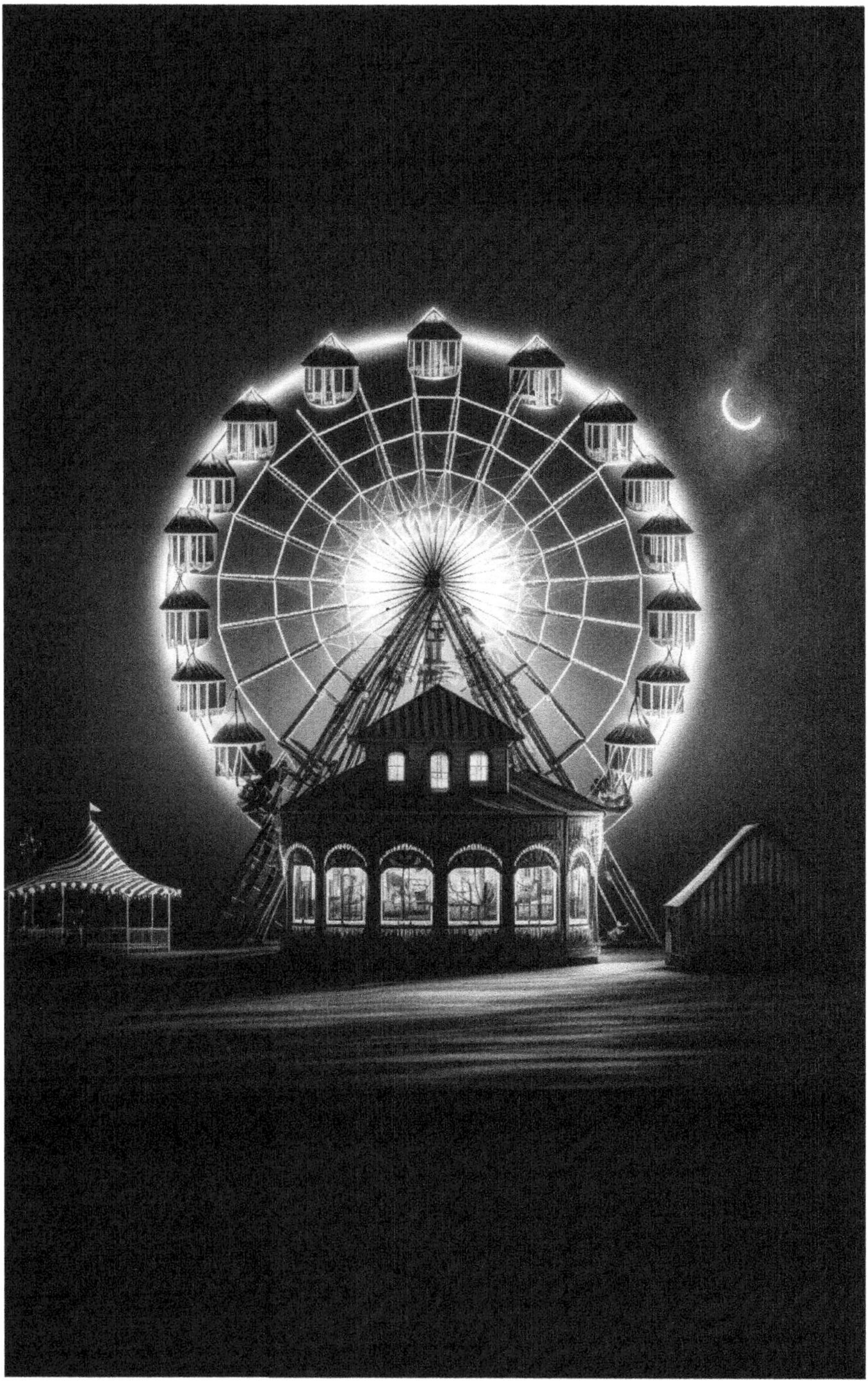

Chapter 1

As I sat in my dark, yet cosy little office, the summer rain was streaming down my window like tears on tax return day - what was left of the daylight now a memory, as the neon flashed its rainbow patches onto my office walls. I sat back in my chair, lit my last Lucky, and was thinking of heading home to the cat, when...in she came. The subtlest of taps on the door blending with the tapping rain were quite unnoticed, and as the door opened, she shimmied into the room and settled in the chair opposite.

"Take a seat," I said belatedly.

The dame was dressed in a silk, emerald green dress, which shimmered in the neon that spilt through the window over the ripples of smooth fabric. She wore a small, green, feathered hat at an angle on her head and she had the look of greenbacks. She stared at me with eyes as green as everything else. The skin she revealed was like peaches and cream, as smooth as wax. She crossed her slim, coltish pins, and I was already caught in whatever trap she had made for me.

"Thanks for agreeing to see me so late detective."

"That's fine," I replied. I was tempted to tell her that I lived by night, but let the thought pass.

"I got a proposition for you, Mr Mitchell," she purred, sensually flicking back honey blonde hair from her petulant face. "My ex-husband is currently on a slab in the local morgue, a bed he made for himself. He was killed by a business rival it's presumed, but I don't need to know who - the guy clearly did me a big favour."

"Well, what can I do for you then Mrs Alessi?" I asked, remembering the name from her recent phone call to my office.

"Miss Alessi. Anna Alessi."

Anna leant forward, and handed me a photograph of a young girl. The girl looked about eight or nine years old, had braided blonde hair and was wearing a silk blouse. She had an impish face and wore a small beret.

"You see, detective, the reason I've come to see you is not because of my ex. As I said, he's now a stiff in the municipal morgue, a sweet little bullet lodged in his head. And he won't be missed, by anyone let alone by me. But you see," she continued, "he was killed over at Penumbra Park two nights ago. You know, where they have the funfair across the bay?"

"Of course," I replied, the memory of freshly made cotton candy filling my nostrils.

"Well, the thing is, he had my daughter with him, Marci. When we split he got custody and I've not seen much of her since."

"Do you mind if we talk somewhere more comfortable?" I asked my client.

"Sure thing, detective."

We made our way down to the lobby via the old Victorian lift, which squealed like a remorseless snitch, eventually landing unceremoniously in the hallway. I took Anna to a bar across the street called Diablo's, where I liked to refresh. We hurried across the wet road, dodging the slow-moving traffic, through the shallow pools of rain that reflected the lights of cars, bars and gas-lit signs, until we reached the high door of Diablo's in all its art deco finery, and went inside.

I ordered myself a rye, and Miss Alessi a white wine, not too sweet. The bar was a discreet place, with little red velvet-lined sitting booths sheltering customers from eavesdroppers.

"I'll get back to what I was saying," continued Anna. "So Marci, she got separated from my ex just before he was plugged. I learnt from the cops that Mark was seen with her shortly before, but when he bought it he was alone near a shooting gallery. Ironic. My daughter was last seen holding a yellow balloon, and that's the last anyone saw of my little girl. I've come to you Mr Mitchell, because I've heard good things about you. You're good at finding people, and finding them alive."

I pondered to myself that I could only actually find people alive, if they were alive...

"So I'm asking you, can you find her and bring my baby to me?"

"I'll do my best Miss Alessi, you can depend on that."

"Anna, please..."

"But I'll need to know more about Marci. Did she know where you live?"

"God, detective, don't talk of her in the past tense."

Anna took out a handkerchief and wiped her eyes.

"Anna, what I meant was...does she know where you live to be able to find you if she went off on her own?"

"No, Marci doesn't know where I'm holed up see. I decided to stay where my ex couldn't track me down, he is...he was, a dangerous man."

As we talked, the room got fuller as people spilled in to watch the act of the evening. The chanteuse's sultry tones filled the room with melody, just as it was filled with tobacco smoke. Anna went on, telling me about her daughter, how old she was for her years. Young it seemed. And about her ex and his shenanigans. She gave me a retainer, it was more than I would have asked for, but she just placed it in my mitt, and said she'd be in touch. She wanted me to go straight to Penumbra Park tomorrow, and see if I could find some leads that the cops had missed, something I was good at.

I stayed on for a second rye. And a third. The music was as heady as the liquor, but I needed to save my head for the next day's business, so I split before midnight and headed to my apartment which was a few blocks away just up the hill near the cemetery - the only place in this city where the souls ever seemed to be at peace.

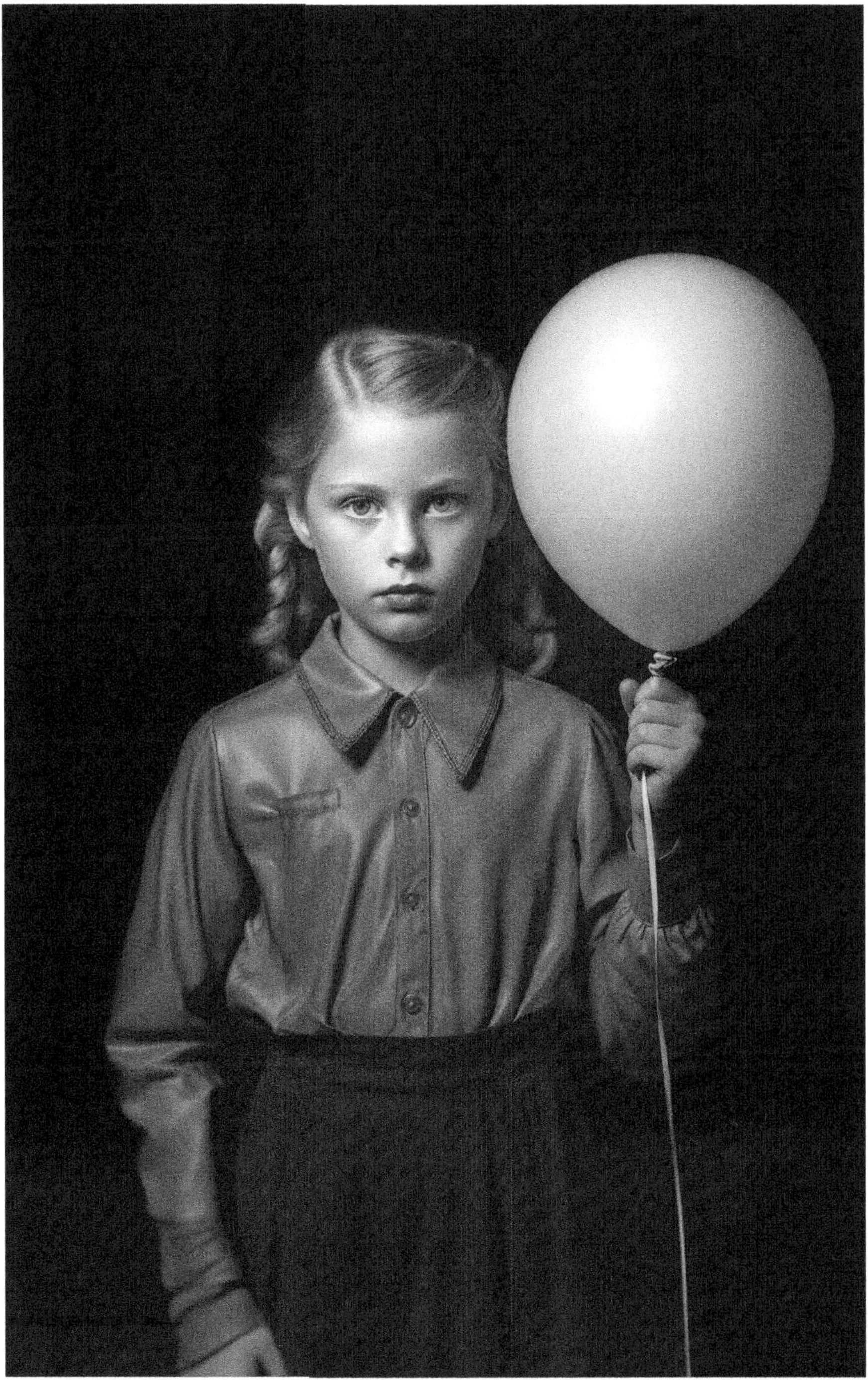

Chapter 2

The rain had stopped, and as I made my way back to my apartment on foot, my fuzzy brain was processing the information Anna had fed me about her ex-husband. Ex in every sense of the word.

She'd hit me with stories of his business dealings, and who might have prepped him for a coffin over at the funfair. She'd said that the cops weren't too interested in finding the killer, on account of the kind of man Alessi was, but that they'd barely shown any more interest in finding her daughter. I finally came to the front door, wishing I'd whistled that passing taxi cab, a little out of puff due to my increasing cigarette intake and waistline, but sharper than when I stepped out of Diablo's.

It was a mild June night, and the sound of crickets cut through the humid air, which was spiked with the scent of honeysuckle. The apartments were compact but modern, on the edge of the main town area, with the cemetery on one side and parkland on the other. I fumbled to find my key, then scratching around the keyhole finally found my purchase and unlocked my apartment door. Buddy greeted me, rubbing against my ankles and mewing. I let him out the kitchen window to slay some mice, and settled down with my last smoke of the day.

The apartment had a man's touch. There were newspapers on the couch, an overflowing ashtray on the coffee table and a sink full of dirty crocks. Still, despite the disarray I was happy with how I'd added a touch of style to the place. The modernist lamp was from Fischer's in town, the plush suite was left to me by my great aunt who was always fond of me, despite me being a pain in the ass. The wallpaper needed an upgrade but still pleased me. The kitchen had all its mod cons, bought with my tax free takings over the last few years. As a good detective I was always busy in Carnock City, where the law was bent, vice aplenty, and your innocence was gone by the time you could string two words together. I knew what had to be done, so I emptied the spent stubs, washed up, and hit the hay.

I sank into a deep sleep, and then into a dream - induced by the alcohol, and the whiff of honeysuckle coming in through the vents from outside. I was in Penumbra Park already, and it was night. All the funfair attractions were in full swing - the carousel with its wild horses and their inflated, feverish nostrils, the kiddie's rides - spinning faster than a dime on a bar table, and the ghost train with its relentless screams and the sound of cars on tracks. There was the clairvoyant's tent, open at the front, with a light on the crystal ball. It sat on a small table, glowing like a prism and diffusing every colour of light, even a few I'd never seen before. There was the shooting gallery, with its battered metallic ducks, clanging as pellets mercilessly ripped through them.

But there were no people. No children, no carnies, and I could only hear the deafening sounds from the illuminated attractions and pools of darkness around them. The deepest, darkest pool was in the centre of all the chaos.

Then a spotlight appeared in a flash.

Where once there was but an inky blackness, appeared a little girl with blonde braids standing bolt upright holding a yellow balloon, staring into my soul. She looked at me like I didn't care. Like she thought I couldn't, wouldn't help her. She suddenly looked upwards into the zenith of the oily sky, and I noticed her feet looked different. I could see the tops of her shoes as her heels lifted off the ground and she was on her tiptoes. Then her toes left the ground, and the balloon took her upwards. I watched her rising slowly into the sky, getting smaller and smaller until all I could make out was a little yellow dot, and then...nothing.

Suddenly all the machines, the screaming, the shooting, the crying, the laughing, all stopped dead in a violent moment. One by one the lights of the attractions went off.

Clang!

Clang!

Clang!

And then there was nothing at all. Nothing to see. Nothing to hear. I could just faintly smell the cotton candy again, but even that went away, fading like smoke from a gun. I was completely alone in an absolute void. I couldn't even feel my body. I wasn't aware of my own breathing, I couldn't remember who I was. Was this real? Was I real? This big nothing went away as I woke up suddenly in a cold sweat, sitting upright in my bed clutching the sheets. Everything was as dark as the dream.

My heart slowed, and I started to breathe again. My body relaxed and my mad grip loosened.

Bang!

Suddenly a light came on. The girl was there again, Marci Alessi. This time she was sitting cross-legged on my bed, still holding that shiny yellow balloon. Her mouth opened wide producing relentless shrieks of depraved laughter. I was confused. I was horrified. Then I really woke up, and it was morning.

It took me a while to feel I was back in the real world, but I felt that dream would be etched on my brain forever. I got ready and headed out.

Before I went to Penumbra Park I knew I had work to do, so I got a cab to the library in town where they had a room full of new microfiche machines where I could do some homework and find out if Anna was straight up. My tired eyes went through the newspapers of the last two days (as the shooting had happened two nights before) and scoured every inch of type for information, also looking for anything relating to Alessi's dealings in business sections. I knew that finding the killer was the best lead I had in finding the girl right now. I drew blanks.

I needed to head down to the crime scene and start asking questions, getting first-hand accounts, and looking for clues. The city cops were as useful as a bribe to a nun, but I did have one contact in the police - an old friend by the name of Vincent Furioni, and I'd arranged that morning to meet up with Vince over at the park to see if he could feed me any leads. So I took a cab to the pier off the end of Renswick Avenue and got myself a ride across the water to the funfair.

I sat on the ferry watching the cityscape get smaller, the buildings get shorter, and the hustle and bustle of the metropolis fall behind. I turned around to see Penumbra Park up ahead, with its Ferris wheel and rides, and the small island's sandy beach beneath the rocky cliff paths that twisted up to the delights above. A wide, modern road swept up the hill on the right side of the cliffs, which I guess is how they got the Ferris wheel up there. Being on foot I took one of the cliff paths until I reached the summit. I headed to where I was to meet up with Vince at the Skittles Lounge Cafe at the rear of the park. When I got there, my friend already had a half-finished coffee, and two spent stubs in his ashtray.

"Brix! So good to see you! Been way too long!" said Vince, grabbing my hand firmly and wildly shaking it.

"It has Vince! We really should catch up outside of discussing cases sometime."

"Of course, you're always welcome to come and see me and the missus, you know where we live."

"Yes, of course Vince. How are Bella, and the kids?"

"All good Brix, I'm a lucky guy."

"So, what have you got on the Alessi case?"

"Not much," he replied, "but I do have a lead. You see..." he went on, "the bullet found in the stiff's skull, it's not one from a gun used commonly by hoods, in fact it took the guys from ballistics quite a while to find the make of the pistol."

"I'm listening..."

"Well, it's from a really old French gun, a nineteenth century percussion pistol - not the kind you'd expect a gangster to be waving around. A real collector's item. So if you can find a keen gun collector you might get your man."

"What about the girl? Anything on her?"

"Nope. Not a scent, Brix. Two or three people saw a girl with a yellow balloon, but no reports since."

We finished our brews. I thanked Vince and he left to get back to the mainland. I began my exploration of the island.

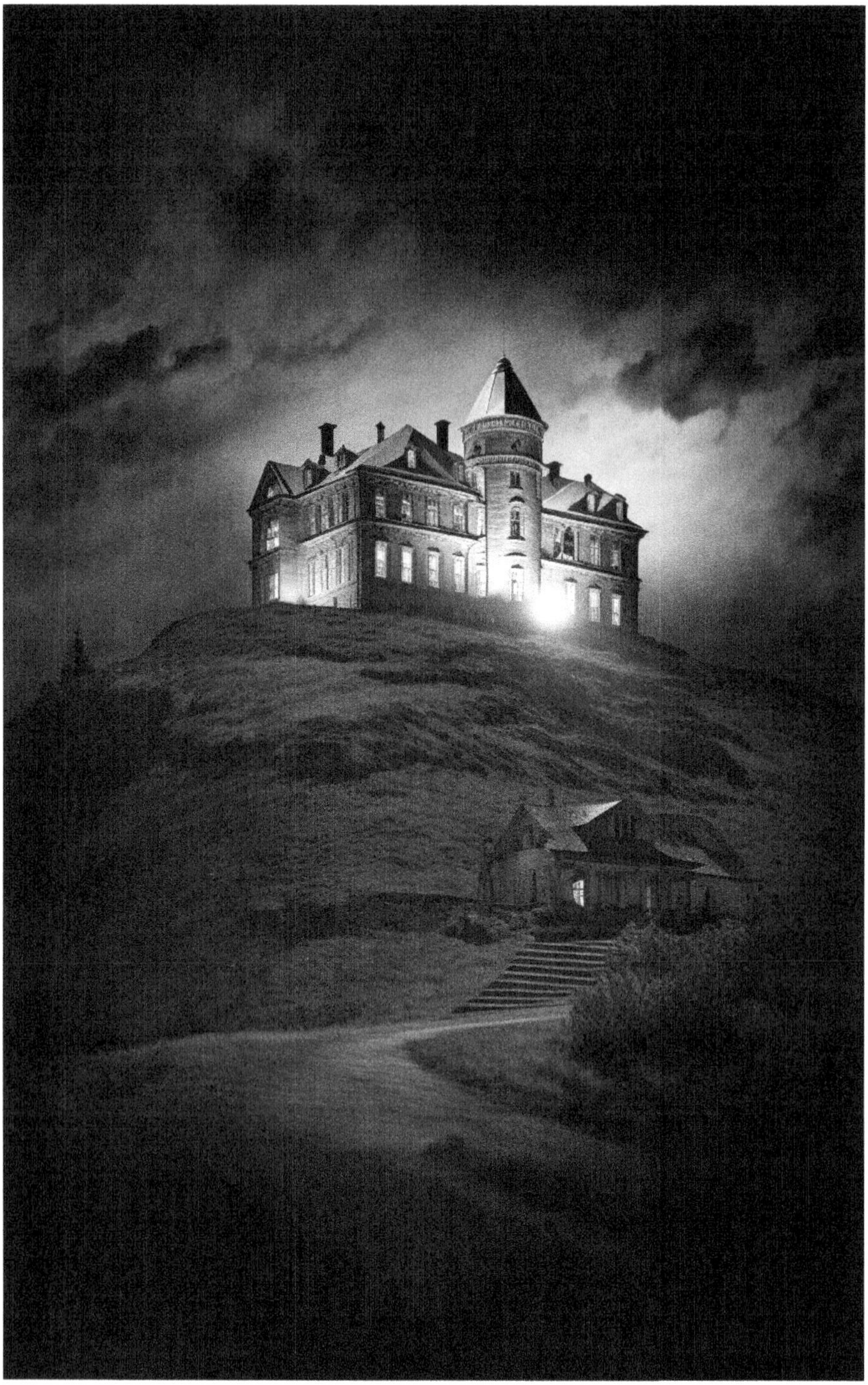

Chapter 3

I headed into the fairground to try and pry open a few leads. There were a number of carnies milling about, as well as a few members of the public having a mooch before the fair opened. There was a carny on the carousel, polishing up the brass rods the horses had lodged in their poor backs. He was about forty-five, and his hair was a pool of black dye. Some of the dye had trickled down his temples. Maybe he didn't know. The irises of his eyes were just as black.

"Excuse me bud, can I ask if you've seen this girl around?" I asked, taking the photograph of Marci from my top pocket and waving it in his direction. The guy squinted his black eyes at the photo.

"You'll have to get up here. I can't see nothing from here pal."

I found the steps around the other side of the ride and got aboard, weaving myself between the equinery. I showed him the photo again.

"Nope. Who is she?"

"A girl who went missing here, after the recent murder."

"Nasty business. I heard the gunshot. I didn't see the girl, but there were so many people that night. The next night they closed us down for investigations, but, the show's gotta go on ain't it?"

"I guess so. Thanks."

I left the guy to get on with his work and spoke to a few more carnies, who were different degrees of polite, as I got nearer to the murder scene. The site was no longer roped off. Less than two days later and not a trace that anything criminal had happened - apart from the hotdog prices. I noticed the unattended change booth was close to the clairvoyant's pitch. I could see a light inside the tent, so I went in. This was the tent from my dream, only a little different. Over the years there had been several soothsayers up here. This one was Madam Future, and she was applying her makeup in thick layers.

"Sorry to disturb. Did you see this girl the night of the murder? She's missing."

Madame Future raised one eyebrow in a mysterious manner.

"Hmmm," she added. "I certainly did."

"Didn't you tell the police ma'am?"

"They never asked me! Why would they? Darn police wouldn't wanna speak to no carny. And I wouldn't wanna speak to no cops. You ain't no cop? You a relation? You ain't no damn reporter?"

"I'm a Private Investigator, ma'am, working on behalf of a client. Anything you can tell me may be useful."

I gave the old sage an incentive from my pocket.

"Well, she came here for a readin' with her mother didn't she?"

"Her mother?"

"She was with a woman. Youngish. She had these shades on and a hat. I couldn't see much of her."

"Was she blonde, brunette, fiery?"

"I don't remember. She was slim. She looked kinda mysterious mister, and that's comin' from me!" she cackled.

Madam Future looked exactly how one imagines an old gypsy sage to appear. Her face was weathered and ruddy, but her eyes were bright blue and alive despite a white rim around her irises from her advanced age. Her pupils were oddly constricted and small, giving her a piercing expression. Her cheekbones were dangerously sharp and there were a few gold teeth framed by poorly applied lipstick. Two rings clung to her right nostril and she wore a headscarf, earrings in every part of each lobe, and an old multi-coloured shawl. She had long fingernails on the end of gnarled fingers adorned with large exotic rings. There were bangles on her arms, the tattoo of a dragonfly on her right lower arm, and what looked like a beetle or scarab on the other, hard to tell with her skin being so wrinkled.

"Is there anything else you can tell me about the woman? Did she have an accent? What was her voice like?"

"Didn't pay much attention to her voice mister, sorry 'bout that."

"And how long was this before the shooting?"

"Not long before the murder. The strangest thing happened. I was just at the end of my tarot readin' exercise. Would ya believe I turned over a disturbin' sequence of cards, but would never have told the little girl? Well, I heard a whistle, a guy whistlin', and then the curtains opened a bit, and an arm came in holdin' a balloon. The woman took the balloon, and gave it the little girl. She then told me she'd gotta go, she'd paid already, see?"

"A yellow balloon?"

"Yes! I'm colour blind you know. Rare for a woman. But we can all see yeller, even us of impaired vision. My mental vision ain't impaired though, that's most sharp mister!"

"And then?"

"I was tidyin' up ma' table, and gettin' ready for the next customer and that's when I heard the commotion. I heard all the screamin' and seen the sides of ma' tent almost cave in, with all the people runnin' away from somethin'. I was really stirred. I couldn't imagine what happened. Soon found out. Never known nothin' like it. Been here goin' on seven years and nothin' like that happened before. Shockin'. Would you like me to give you a readin'? On the house mister."

Although I knew it was hokum, the old woman had been very helpful, and as her grin seemed almost coquettish, I obliged her.

She sat there mysteriously waving her disfigured hands over the smooth, illuminated globe on her chestnut table. Her eyes were closed in concentration, and after enough time for the future to catch up with us, her vivid eyes burst open and stared into the sphere.

"I see a place. A mysterious place. At night. Let me focus."

She placed her hand on her furrowed brow for a moment, and then clasped her hands together with a wide grin.

"It's a big old house, on a hill. There are many windows. The house is full of pain."

I listened, starting to actually get into it.

"There is a light in one of the upstairs rooms, and I see a woman. She looks...lonely."

It sounded intriguing, but I really had to split.

"Thank you Madam Future, that's quite the gift you have, but I really have to get going."

"But there is more... Damn! It's gone! You upset the mind flow mister, you shouldn't do that durin' a readin'!"

I apologized and thanked the old girl. I now knew that the balloon was a signal, and that Marci was with someone, this mysterious dame with the hat and shades. Find this woman and I'd find the killer, and the girl. But would I find her alive? I needed to get back to Anna Alessi and tell her what I'd found out.

The sun was heading behind the clouds, and folk started coming into the fairground. The change booth was now manned by a youngster whose spectacles looked so thick and prescribed they made his eyes look small like piss holes in the snow. I asked if he remembered the girl. He didn't. Then it turns out he wasn't even working on the night of the murder.

Now that I guessed the killer had taken the girl, and had an accomplice, I was keen to find out Mark Alessi's enemies, who were countless according to Anna. The only shred of physical evidence was the little French bullet that had been dislodged from the cadaverous brow of Mark Alessi. It was a fascinating lead for the killer to leave. I was intrigued to know more. I needed to get back to my office and check my messages, so headed off.

I took the same route back down the quietest cliff path, which was obscured from the others by overhanging rocky crags. The sun disappeared behind the cliff top as I descended, leaving the path in shadow. A family approached and I stepped into the little passing space to give them room, and then there was no one in sight but a guy around halfway down in a black coat with his collar up high, smoking a cigarette and looking out to the bay. In his other hand, he had what looked like a piece of fried chicken, and he was having a good munch on this between drags. This guy looked a might suspicious, and I stayed put and lit my own. The stranger kept on looking out to the water and slowly taking drags, and I was just weighing up my options when I felt something wedged in my back, the unmistakable feel of a hard, very modern revolver barrel.

"This is a message for you de...tective."

I stopped breathing just then.

"Quit sticking your nose in other people's business, and you might live to see another day. But if you don't, you'll be at the bottom of that bay with a pair of concrete boots. Understood?"

I figured the dark-coated guy was Gun Happy's accomplice. I had to think this one through, quick. The accomplice threw his smoke down with contempt, and turned and faced me with his arms crossed, equally contemptuously. He still had the greasy snack in his left hand, poking out from his crossed arms.

"And it needs two of you, and a piece, to tell me this?" I enquired.

"I don't need no discussion, you nosey little asshole..." said the dope behind me.

"I ain't little you creep!"

The two of them walked me down the steps, one behind with his rod in my back, and one in front with his right hand in his pocket - and I guessed he wasn't keeping candies in there. His left still clutched what was left of his snack.

I realised that the slightest move and I could get my spinal cord ripped in a second. Suddenly two boys, screaming and laughing in excitement brushed past us on their way down. I felt the pressure of the barrel release from my back as the mug behind me got distracted. Thank God he wasn't that spooked, otherwise someone would have been worm food. We continued down the steps. It was quiet now the boys had gone away.

Suddenly, out of the blue, a huge gull swooped down to steal the piece of fried chicken from the left hand of the mug in front. He completely freaked and was flapping about like a maniac. The sap behind me pulled his gun away from my back and I felt a rush of air past my face as he aimed at the gull. In that instant I forged my right hand into a cutting weapon, and sliced behind me it at his head, knocking him down. Before he had the chance to evaluate, I'd kicked the revolver from his hand and it disappeared over the railings, way out of reach. I dropped down low and grabbed my colt from its holster on my lower leg and immediately turned and shot at the legs of the sap in front of me, sending him crashing down towards the bay. I suspected in pieces. I smashed the butt of my gun into the other's dumb head, and ran up the path and its steps until I was at the top, my thigh muscles were burning and my lungs were as flat as a shot tyre.

Being a June evening, there was no cover of darkness, and I had no ride, but spotted a taxi and the driver was happy to help when I bunged her a note. The cab took me down to the ferry point, and I stayed in the cab until the ferry came. On board, I lit my last smoke and looked around for trouble. When I was satisfied there was none, I pulled my hat down over my eyes and I stayed like that, blanking out the evening, until the boat pulled up at the pier, paid, and disembarked.

I made my way to my office, and warily entered. There were a couple of messages. The important one was from Anna. She wanted me to go down to her apartment in the valley and give her a progress report. I couldn't call her to say it wasn't safe, as I didn't have her number, so headed to my rented garage and drove down to the valley. I was there by about 9pm, constantly checking the rear view mirror for any knuckleheads tailing me. I parked around the corner and walked down to her apartment block.

It was a set of apartments in the old Spanish-style. Very nice. I cased the place before my finger met with the number 12 buzzer.

"Detective!" she exclaimed.

Thank God the dame was still alive.

"Please come!" she purred.

The front door unlatched and I went upstairs to find her at her door. She let me in. Her apartment was spacious and modernist, like something from a Fred and Ginger flick. It was decorated with wall art, of which there were several paintings, modern art pieces by various names. A couple were vaguely familiar, but then I'm no collector. There were works signed by Catherine March, Jean Henry, Mary Meredith, Louise Patterson and Geoffrey Carroll. There were also several sculptures including a ballerina in a Degas pose in the rough-hewn style of Jacob Epstein.

Anna offered me a seat. The coffee table in front was a mess. There were fashion and art magazines, shot glasses with Mexican motifs, makeup including a strange white lipstick, a letter and some jewellery. In contrast, Anna looked immaculate. I was as spellbound by her as I'd been the very first time we'd met. But she'd already hooked me. This time Anna was more business-like. She wore an immaculate white trouser suit with a simple necklace of ebony beads. Her hair was fashioned up in a bun, and she focused on me with those incredible green peepers.

"Scotch?"

"I'll take it. Thanks."

"What did you find detective? Any leads on my baby?"

"I found more than I bargained for. I found a couple of dumbbells who could have easily finished me on my way back from the crime scene. They warned me off the case."

"Oh God! I had no idea. Look, if you think the whole thing is too dangerous? But please, I need to find my daughter, anything could have happened to her."

I was tempted to tell her danger was my middle name, just as I took a twitchy peep through the curtains to check for anything suspicious outside.

"I'm not a quitter Anna. If your girl is findable, I'll find her."

Anna began to crack, and tears flowed down over her soft cheeks into the corners of her mouth. I consoled her. I could only imagine what it felt like to have a missing child as I had no kids of my own. She then curled up on the sofa, and I offered her a cigarette, which she took and drew every last drop of nicotine from it.

Then I filled her in about my afternoon at Penumbra Park, the strange woman, the mysterious arm with the balloon, the tip off about the French gun from my anonymous source.

"So, we need to find this killer, and their accomplice. I need to know everything you can tell me about your husband you haven't already, and who you think might have a motive outside of the usual gang-related feuds. That's my hunch. It's not gang-related. It's more personal than that."

I settled down with my second scotch, and Anna gave me an abridged account of her ex-husband's life, from when he was a kid up to his recent demise. He was bought up in a dirt poor tenement-style block downtown during the depression. He got involved with a local gang, and with his physical presence and entrepreneurial skills he became quite the big hoodlum. But she said there were plenty of skeletons in his closet. She met him when she was eighteen, and he early thirties, around a decade ago, and claimed she didn't know of his reputation or exploits, but fell for him. For years she'd put up with his womanizing, and tried to ignore his misdemeanours.

Alessi had made many enemies in his life, but most of them were no longer breathing. Along with enemies he'd had many people in the palm of his hand, including members of the force and other civil servants. He was the overlord of his own empire, but few actually knew what Alessi looked like outside his closest associates. His profile was as low as his morals, and when he did venture out he went to places that were very discreet for the price of protection. He was a man who constantly changed his appearance. She said his hair, his clothes, all changed from season to season. Many of the men who worked for him wouldn't recognise him in the broad daylight of Main Street, let alone a dark alley downtown.

She knew she'd lived on his blood money, and still was, although it was almost run out. I then thought of my retainer, it too was blood stained. I had to find this little girl, and it would all be worth it. I knew that the French bullet could be the key to it all. I told Anna I'd visit the city museum and see if I could get some clues. She thanked me and shook my hand firmly. I stepped into the night. This time I had Anna's number, but calling her had to be a last resort, I had no clue if the phone was tapped. I drove back to my apartment and it was lights out.

I dreamt again that night. I thought of Madam Future's prediction in her crystal ball. The old mansion on the hill in the darkness. A solitary figure silhouetted in the window. The heavy rain crashed down on the old roof and cascaded down the side of the hill. The water swelled and carried me down to the sea, where the ocean swallowed me up whole.

That's all I can remember, but I woke feeling quite fresh, not a bit salty, got ready. There was work to be done.

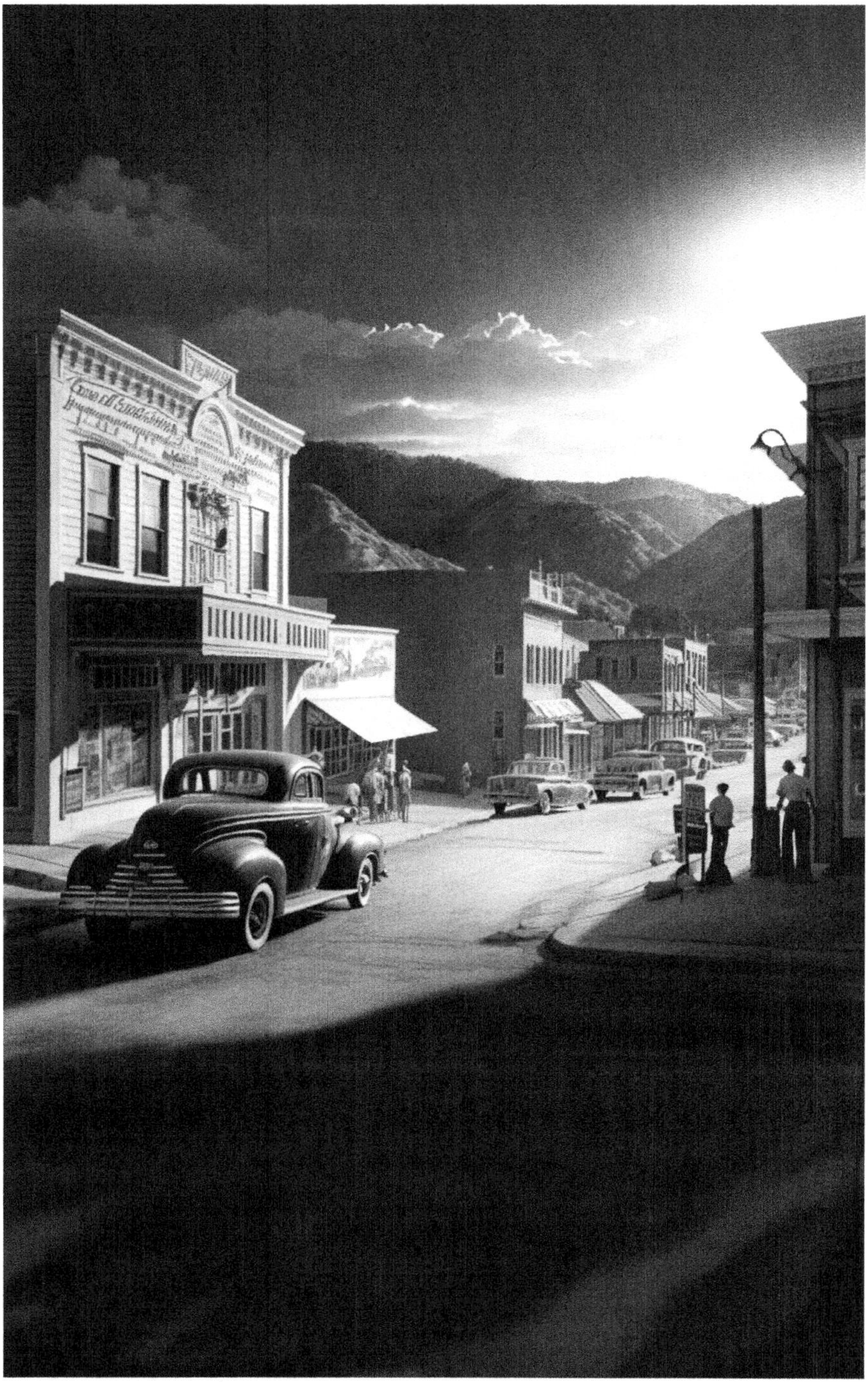

Chapter 4

Next day was Thursday, and I made a beeline for the museum. The Central Carnock Museum had a Georgian-style facade, which made me think of home - that is my old home. Until I was about six years old I lived in a small town on the outskirts of London. I'd been back to my hometown since, and remember seeing a lot of buildings like this. My mother was from a place called Devonshire, and she died when I was a young kid. I don't remember much of her. My father brought me to the States and he worked on the docks as a manager. It was a very different scene to back in the Home Counties and it was before the depression hit. The city was a strange, exhilarating place, but we lived in a decent terrace on the outskirts of town.

I joined the police as a rookie just as the crime wave hit, and they needed all the manpower they could muster. But the stench of greed and corruption wafted into every corner of the city and nowhere could escape it, not even the church or the law itself. I served my years and earned my badge, but lone wolf was really the only future I could see. I'd made some bad choices, but I'd learned hard lessons and wanted a clean slate. Private Dick was the route I chose. It was a rocky road, but the only way I could see through the fog.

It was a clear, bright day in midtown. The asphalt was burning in the sun's rays, which cast deep shadows across parts of the busy street which was bustling with traffic and pedestrians. I walked up the dozen or so steps to the revolving doors of the museum. It wasn't that trade was so good they needed revolving doors, but that's what they had. I was swept into a large reception area with nice furniture and a lot of plants. The CCM was a free museum; all its exhibits were donated or loaned by private parties or organizations. The guy who founded the museum left a ton of his own art and collections on the basis that the place remained free access to the public.

I went up to the desk and was greeted by a geeky-looking chick in a blue cardigan who smiled earnestly at me - at once sincere, unlike some of the shop girls and boys in town with their Bakelite smiles. Her hair was tied back and she wore horn-rimmed glasses. She had a name badge. It had "Dorothy" on it.

"Hello sir, have you come to look around our wonderful museum?"

"Hi miss," I said, avoiding using her badge name, which always seems trite when it's damn obvious one can read. "It's a beautiful building. But I'm mainly interested in your armory. Do you have a section with antique weaponry?"

"Of course, sir. We have weaponry on the third floor, from Roman times to the end of the last century, both European and American. We also have American Indian weapons. Is there anything in particular that piques your interest, sir?"

"Well, I might be clutching at straws, but I wondered if I could speak to someone who specializes in old European pistols. I'd like to know if there are any collectors in the city, perhaps someone has ever donated antique pistols?"

Dorothy looked at me and her wide eyes got wider.

"Why do you ask?" she enquired.

"I'll cut to the chase, I'm a private detective, and an antique pistol was used recently in a crime. I'm very keen to trace who used it."

"Really?" she said, with a look of astonishment. Had I said something wrong?

"Was it by any chance a nineteenth-century French percussion pistol of the flintlock variety sir?"

I could feel my heart rate quickening in my chest, fighting to burst from my rib cage.

"Well, yes!" I exclaimed. I was in shock at her impossible knowledge, as such details were yet to break.

"Come with me Mr..."

"Mitchell. Brixham Mitchell."

Dorothy locked the front door of the joint while she was away from her post, and led me to an elevator in the corner of the reception area. I was struck by the bright red elevator door and its elongated star shaped window, framed in gold leaf - more modern than the museum's facade. Dorothy hit the button for the third floor and we stood in opposite corners.

"I don't really need these," she stated.

"Need what?"

"The glasses. Only for reading. They are good for the image though," she laughed, nervously.

Dorothy removed her horn rims and undid her hair. It flowed magnificently over her shoulders. Her eyes became limpid pools I wanted to bathe in.

"Well, hello!" I thought, as my heart raced like Jesse Owens on a promise. In a city with such ugliness in every corner, a little beauty went a long way. It seemed Dorothy also had quite the modern look under that old-fashioned receptionist shtick.

"This all sounds very intriguing," she said, a little flush of cheek.

"I'm more than intrigued," I replied.

Dorothy slid out of the lift and I followed her, like the big bad wolf, or maybe a puppy on a tidbits promise. The museum was huge. We walked through two rooms full of antiques, past visitors, and a guard who nodded as we passed. We entered a room full to the hilt with weaponry. There were spears and slingshots on the walls, cabinets full of devilish-looking knives, and guns aplenty. Dorothy went up to a slim old man with small oval spectacles who appeared to be sleeping in the corner.

"Harold!"

Harold sat bolt upright and awkwardly adjusted his glasses, almost dropping them on the floor.

"This man is a private detective. He would like to ask you about a mid-19th century French percussion pistol. It was used in a crime."

Harold stood up.

"Good Lord! Come with me sir."

Harold led us into a small annex room where there was a large glass cabinet in the centre which held numerous firearms. Near the middle of the cabinet there was a pistol-shaped space in the velvet lining. Under this was a small plaque with "French Flintlock Pistol - circa 1855" scribed on it.

"I'd come here to find out if you knew of a collector or donator of such a pistol! When was it stolen?"

"About a month ago sir," replied Harold. "There were no signs of a break in, but one morning we came into work and the pistol was gone. We presumed it was an inside job, one of the recent security recruits. We couldn't prove anything, but we let them go to be on the safe side."

"I'm speechless," I understated.

"And you say this was used in a crime?" asked Harold, squinting.

"Yes, I need to find who stole this gun. A girl's life could be at stake."

"This gun was donated by a businessman in town. Was it used in a robbery?"

"Worse than that. But, who donated the pistol?"

"Let me go and get the donations and loans book."

Dorothy excused herself and went back downstairs to her reception duties, as Harold fiddled with a large leather-bound tome. "Yes, here it is. It was a Mr..."

Harold squinted again trying to make out the name.

"Alessi. Mark Alessi. Yes, it was a donation. Not a loan."

I was stunned into silence. Mark Alessi had been plugged by his own gun. But why?

"Tell me, Harold, was this reported to the police?"

"It wasn't I'm afraid. Nothing like this had ever happened before and we didn't want to put people off donating and lending us their antiques. The museum thrives on a changing collection through loans and donations. We have signature pieces, but...Good Lord!" uttered Harold, looking me straight in the eyes. "You've just triggered my memory, it's not so good these days, but if it hadn't been for you asking that question, and my feeling of deja vu, I'd never have remembered."

"Yes? Go on Harold, what do you remember?"

"Someone came in some time before the robbery. It could have been weeks or months, I really don't know, and they asked me the same question as you; "Who donated the French pistol?" and I told them. The answer was the same as I'll tell you, Mark Alessi."

"Description? Can you remember Harold? This is the kind of breakthrough I dream of!"

"Yes, it was a young woman, quite plain if I remember. She spoke well and seemed educated. Not the criminal type."

"Well, you never know. Anything else? Think Harold, think!"

"She had a jacket on with a crest."

"A crest?"

"Yes, like a family crest. There were lions on it. No. Not lions."

"Not lions. Think Harold!"

"I think it was horses, and...fish? Sorry sir, that sounds vague but I really can't remember. But there was definitely a crest. With creatures."

"Thank you Harold. How many security men did you let go?"

"Two."

"Do you have their details? I'd like to speak to them. The police won't get involved."

"I do have their given names but I have no idea where they live, it's a big city and they could be anywhere."

So all I had to go on was the woman, and an old man's dubious memory of a family crest.

"You've been a big help Harold," I said, handing him my card. "Hit me up if you remember anything else, or if any colleagues can help. Do you have a local history department?"

"I'm afraid not, you'll need the central library for that sir."

I took the lift down to the foyer and saw Dorothy again. She was talking to a customer but took the time to glance in my direction and gave me a little nod of approval which I returned with a corny salute. The library was about half a mile west, and I headed briskly up the sidewalk until I reached the white, deco-styled palace of knowledge. I browsed the local history of the city and surrounds and eventually found information on prominent families in the area. There was a chapter on each of these pioneering families, and luckily for me, their family crests. About four crests in, I saw it...Jackpot.

The family crest had two mythical figures that were half horse, half fish - like equine mermaids, standing rampant on their spiralling fishy tails on either side of a central illustration of an arm holding a torch with a flame. The family name was "Henry" and the first member of this illustrious clan to sail across the pond was a Donald Marc Henry, who came from a British family of note. In the States he made even more dough by investing in new industries. It was all interesting stuff, but I was keen to get to the present, and skipped swiftly through several generations of the family. The book wasn't too modern though, it was an 1875 edition. I did find that the family seat had remained the same since old Don first made passage to the new world until that date, and it was a grand old pile nestling in the hills upstate, called Cranborough. How the other half live. So, this was presumably where the nosey visitor came from, the woman who asked about the gun, wearing the family crest.

I headed back to my place, had a quick lunch, and refuelled my iron horse. By afternoon, I was heading up-state on the main northern route, thinking about French pistols, mysterious dames, and the vision of an old house on a craggy hill from the musings of an old clairvoyant.

By late afternoon I reached the small town of Fable, which lay at the foot of the hills where the Henry estate was refuted to be, four miles off the main highway. "Fable. Population 894". Only someone had crossed off the "4" and written "3" next to it. My first impressions were that Fable was as different to Carnock City as Dorothy was to a doorman at Diablo's. Quiet and forgotten, a slow pace of life, somewhere where you could lose the world, yet somewhere it was harder to get lost in like a big city. But then it was hard to know if Fable was a thriving place, or if it was dying. Maybe it was hanging on with a vengeance.

There were old factories which looked battered and forgotten. There were stray dogs and a few stray people. But there were nice little businesses, many of them wrapping up for the day. A barbers, shoesmiths, candy store, grocery shop, and at the end of the street on the way out of town there was a little diner that was open for trade. It was a big old silver dining car, advertising tempting junk bites and sodas. There wasn't much passing traffic - I'd guess this was for the locals.

Art's Diner was warmly lit, with a few folk sipping drinks and taking bites out of burgers bigger than their own jaws. Hungry, I went in and ordered chicken and fries with some Java, which hit the right notes. I landed a couple of curious looks from the other diners, but nothing too nasty. I got talking to the guy who ran the joint. Art told me about the Henry family. They never came down into town...at least not on foot. They'd just pass through on their way to other places. He said there was a guy, his sister and an old woman; the matriarch. He wasn't sure if they all lived there. The father had died many years ago. That's all he knew. I told him I was a historian but I'm sure he didn't believe me. Art carried on shining up a glass and didn't seem to care. I guess he was happy to have customers coming to his little off-the-map town.

"We get the kids in after school. They come here for sodas and ice cream and some of them spoil themselves for their dinners, and their mothers ain't happy about that!" he said.

I tossed the old guy a tip, read the local paper, which had nothing about the Alessi case, finished my coffee and left. I went straight to the discreet little guest house Art had tipped me off about called The Ark, booked a room for the night, and changed my clothes into something easier. The guesthouse was adequate. They took my money and left me alone. That was the kind of deal I liked. I rang my pal Vince who was at home with his missus. Although I trusted Vince, I didn't fill him in about the stolen gun, but told him I was in Fable, and that I thought I'd found a link to the Alessi murder at the Henry mansion - which could even lead me to the girl. I figured it was better someone knew where I was, just in case things didn't go to pat.

I walked through town and went past Art's place, heading northwards. The diner was now closed. With the lights off it was like Art had never really existed - a mere figment of my imagination. I went further out of town, and after ten minutes I got to the gas station he'd mentioned, which was still open for business. At least there was somewhere to fill the tank on leaving. Fable hadn't many souls, but the few that lived here needed a lot of gas to get anywhere else. The wind started to pick up a little, and I squashed my trilby down square on my noggin. I got to the little crossroads, and took a path nearby, as Art had advised - the leafy uphill walking route that got to a point with a clear view of Cranborough. You could also see the big, craggy hill it sat on, and the road sweeping up to it.

It was an impressive stately pile, with a central round tower that the west and east wings hung off, three main floors, and more windows than an advent calendar. It was pretty much the vision that Madame Future had described in her crystal ball, and while I knew all that was flapdoodle, I found it such a coincidence it made me certain I was in the right place. If I was a betting man I'd have put my life on it.

Below the house, at the foot of the hill was a small outbuilding with a porch, like you'd use to rent out to people, or where you'd send someone to live if you didn't want them around the main house. I was just thinking about my next move when I saw someone leave the outbuilding and walk around the base of the hill to the right side of the house. I think it was a woman. I was in a sheltered spot with trees all around me, save for the gap allowing my view of the hall. The light was now fading, but the wind had settled.

The house looked ominous and unwelcoming. I stood there smoking a Lucky and pondering my next move. Did I just go in there and ask politely what the hell the lady was doing asking about a gun that was stolen and then used in a murder? Did I pretend I was someone else? As I mused I heard the noise of a car. For a second I wasn't sure whether it was above or below, but then I saw the headlights as it crept down the bend from behind the hill, and came down the dark road. There were two silhouetted figures inside, and as it approached my vantage point I pulled back behind the trees out of sight, and the headlights flooded everywhere around me. After a few moments the car disappeared, but I could still hear its lively motor humming. Then I couldn't hear it anymore but could see the lights sweeping up the road in the direction of the gas station, towards town. I figured nowhere was open now, so maybe they were heading towards Carnock.

I left my hidey hole and made my way to the foot of the hill. There were still lights on, so I guessed someone was home. Under the cover of darkness, I climbed the steps that ran up the hill until I was near the entrance. I decided it was no good breaking and entering at this point, and what exactly was I looking for? I walked forwards and was now fully exposed in bright light, in the middle of an eclipse of moths. The front door had a large metal knocker in the form of the family crest. There was also a small buzzer on the side of the wall. Being a simple man, I chose the buzzer, which seemed to resonate through the big old house.

I waited.

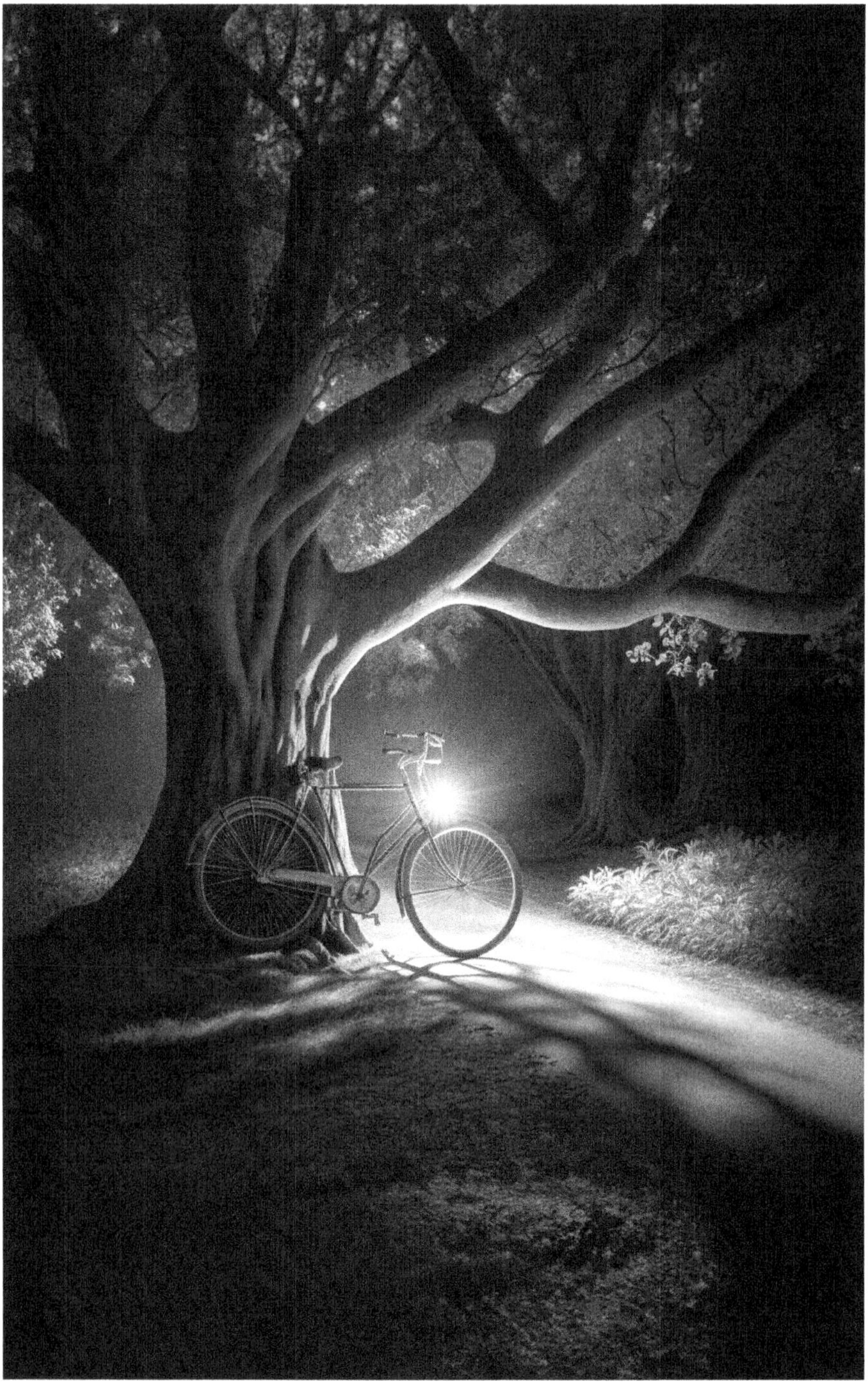

Chapter 5

As I stood in the doorway of the big house, I saw a light turn on inside, and I heard footsteps coming towards me. The grand old door creaked open and a tall, stately man greeted my gaze. The guy must have cut a striking figure in his youth - he still had quite the presence. He was balding, puffy under the eyes, but with strong features and a healthy complexion. He raised his head, just to make sure he was looking down on me that little bit more, and fixed his eyes on me so firmly that I felt like he was reading the thoughts in my head.

"Can I help you sir?"

"I hope so. I'm looking for a young woman who visited the museum in Carnock some months ago. I'm a representative of the museum."

"I'm afraid the young lady of the house has recently left, and won't be returning until tomorrow."

I could just see into the hallway, with its harlequin tiled floor, potted plants and stairway sweeping up.

"Well I'm sorry to have bothered you tonight. Perhaps if I come back to..."

I then heard a low woman's voice from inside.

"Who is it, Hal?" the voice said.

"A man from the museum in Carnock, he's looking for Jean."

Hal stepped aside, as an overweight old woman came into view, shuffling slowly and wincingly with a walking frame. She had a toadish face, a mess of thick grey hair, and was wearing a shawl.

"She's not here, Mr..."

"Mr Summers," I lied.

"She left with her brother, Mr Summers. Are you looking for some information?"

"Yes I am, madam."

"Well, come in, you can talk to me Mr Summers. I'm Martha, come this way."

"But Mrs Henry," I heard Hal whisper, "We're not meant to be having visitors at this time."

"Nonsense, Hallam. I may not get out, but that does not mean I don't like some company for God's sake!"

Martha led me into a grand sitting room. It had windows covered by thick curtains so the room remained lit only by a subdued ceiling light and a couple of table lamps. It was quite the joint, with all the trimmings you'd expect in a hereditary pile, and more to spare. In the centre of the room was an enormous suite, and the room was lined with bureaus, bookcases and cabinets filled with odd collectibles including animal skulls, old relics, African fetish objects and other curios. The wallpaper was green and furry, and looked positively ancient. In the far corner there was a fetching collection of taxidermy animals in a tall display; a badger, a fox, and birds, in a fanciful woodland diorama. A huge gramophone sat in another corner, and there was a vast stone fireplace with dying embers. On the mantelpiece several antique clocks kept perfect time, or at least they all kept the same time, I'd lost track of it myself. There were several paintings, mostly country views, and a tall mirror with a fancy frame, that had turned as green as the wallpaper.

"Take a seat Mr Summers. Can I offer you a beverage? Tea? Scotch?"

"Thank you Mrs Henry, a scotch would be very nice."

"Ice?"

"No thank you, ma'am. You're very kind."

After Hal had poured me a drink and left us alone, Martha sidled up to the sofa and slid into her seat, leaving her walking frame at the side. She was quite puffed out in doing so.

"Don't mind me," she said. "Just getting comfortable."

I saw her struggling with the cushion, so I got up, plumped it for her, and stuck it behind her as she leaned forwards.

"Thank you kindly. So what brings you to Cranborough? We don't get many visitors up here these days. What was it you wanted to know about the estate?"

"Well, we're doing a study of important and historic families in the county ma'am."

"Martha, please!" she ordered, with a twinkle in her eye.

"I'm finding what we have isn't up to date. You see we have lots of information about older generations of the Henrys, but not so much in the last few generations."

"Well, that's very much my lifetime. I'm seventy-five years old. And I wasn't always a cripple you know."

"No," I replied as if I knew all about the woman.

"Well, I've been like this since I was around fifty, before that I was half the weight, I rode horses, I played tennis. I was quite the athlete. But it's not something easy to talk about."

"Of course," I sympathized.

I was dead curious, but couldn't push her further.

"I'm sure you were."

"Yes, we may have privilege, but we've never been idle. Do you know I was also quite the looker in my day? Some say I still am," she said, coyly.

She reached into a drawer which was set in the table between us, and produced an old photograph of her as a young woman. She was very handsome back then. She smiled at me and put the photo back.

"Hal!" she suddenly exclaimed, not at all coyly. Hal entered the room very quickly, as if he'd been just outside the door the whole time. "Can you stoke the fire for our guest?"

I waited for Hal to finish what he was doing, and leave us.

"Hallam is my companion here. I'll let you into a secret, he's not really a valet, but he looks after me," she chuckled, and as she did a stream of perspiration ran down her forehead, and she dabbed it with an oversized silk handkerchief.

"I lived here with my beloved Francis. We lost him years ago. I have one daughter and a son. My daughter still lives here in the east wing, and my son stays whenever he wants. The house is way too big for me alone."

"I think I may have seen them earlier drive past me on my way up?"

"Yes, they were going into Carnock. My son Johnny runs a mineral business. My daughter Jean works from home, she's an artist. She exhibits you know. We all do what we can for charities also."

"Do you have a charity close to your heart?" I asked, without the slightest interest in anything but building some rapport.

"The charity for stroke victims, it rehabilitates the poor souls. My husband was struck by one and he never had the chance to be rehabilitated. There has been tragedy in this family. I hope such misfortune never befalls my children."

Martha had a look of deep sorrow in her dark eyes.

"Jean goes into the city quite often to sell her art. She exhibits at a gallery there - The Mocata."

"I know it," I replied. The Mocata was one of several museums in Carnock. - The Museum of Contemporary and Traditional Art - which had a gallery for regional artists.

Martha talked about her children, about their lives, and about her late husband. She talked about the house, how much the upkeep cost them, and how they weren't wealthy anymore. How she had no grandchildren, which troubled her. We talked for a while until the fire was again embers. Martha began to tire and called Hal in to make her more comfortable. I couldn't really get to the point and ask what her daughter was doing asking about a pistol that was later stolen and then used in a murder followed by a child abduction.

"I think ma'am is too tired to carry on Mr Summers," Hal advised.

At this point, Martha had drifted off, and I nodded, thanking Hal. But very suddenly Martha came to. She sat up quite violently. I was still there on the chair opposite. Her face was pale and bluish, her eyes were fixed on me, and her lips quivered.

"Hal!" she called to her companion.

"Who is this man? Has he come to get the girl?"

The girl? Could she mean...?

Hal asked me to leave; "I'm sorry sir, but Martha is having one of her episodes. I think she's exhausted herself today, I'll see you out."

"I don't want him here!" she exclaimed, turning away from me and extending her bony fingers in my direction.

"He's...nosey!"

"I'm so sorry Mrs Henry, do forgive me, I hope you remember our conversation later."

By now the old girl was flapping her arms about in agitation, and I knew it really was time to get the hell out of there. Poor woman. Hal led me to the hallway, and I stepped out into the darkness of the night. I took the steps down, which were lit just enough to avoid me snapping my neck. What did Mrs Henry mean when she'd said "The girl"? It could have just been a delirious outburst. But what if during that episode she'd been more candid than in our whole conversation? That fusty old house would leave a lasting impression with me I'm sure, and the look of feverish fear when old Martha looked into my eyes might stick around for longer. I made my way to the centre of town, and to the little guesthouse. I had no interest in staying overnight now, I wanted to get the hell back home and plan my next move. My motor was parked just around the back.

I took my keys out to put them in the door of my Ford. Next thing I knew, I had that familiar feeling of the end of a hard gun barrel wedged firmly into my spine. As the man grabbed my arm, the end of the gun slid into my right side, and lodged just under my ribs. His other paw went straight for the gun holstered on my leg. He knew where to find it alright.

"Get in the car and drive. No drama, just do it," he spat.

Refusing didn't seem a viable option with only a gun barrel between a piece of burning lead and my soft insides. The sound of his voice had a familiar ring to it, in fact I think I'd heard it on a cliff path quite recently. Yes, this mug didn't give up. At least this time his dumb sidekick didn't seem to be around, maybe that one had learnt his lesson. As I drove away Gun Happy kept pointing the rod at me from the passenger seat.

"What's your angle?" I enquired.

"Shut it! Keep your trap shut and drive!"

We were soon on the road to the main highway, which weaved through trees, and eventually straightened up as it came to a T junction just before the highway itself.

"Turn left here! Slowly!" Gun Happy urged.

We went down a narrower track, where there were signs to a quarry. Danger signs.

"Park here!" he ordered, after I'd driven about half a mile down the dark track.

I pulled up, sharpish, and the mug's head jolted forward.

"Hey! No funny business! Get out!"

He followed me out of the driver's door, with the piece still pointed at me. I noticed in the corner of my eye that there was a bicycle parked nearby. I figured Gun Happy wasn't planning on taking my car back to town with him and this was his ride.

"You're gonna have a little accident right here!" he enlightened me.

He let out an insane giggle. The freak surely enjoyed his work. He stuck the barrel in me again this time into my ribs. I winced. He cackled again. He took me to the edge of what I guessed was a sheer drop. The precipice was lit by the car headlights, only I couldn't see the bottom of the quarry, just inky blackness. He then stepped back, away from me - I heard his footsteps in the gravel, loud then quieter.

"Hands up! Now, you don't know how deep that fall is do you mister? But at least you got a chance. If you're full of lead, you ain't got a chance in hell!"

Gun Happy talked sense. But if he filled me full of lead it wouldn't look like an accident now would it? He wanted me to jump alright.

I shuffled a little to my left. As I did, I dislodged a small rock that rolled over the edge. I waited to hear the sound of it hitting the ground. Disappointingly I heard nothing.

"Stay the hell where you are!" he screamed.

Next thing I knew; my foot was burning as he let two shots ring out. This was serious. I had no options left; I knew he was gutless enough to plug me if I didn't obey.

I hopped off the edge and disappeared into the dark emptiness.

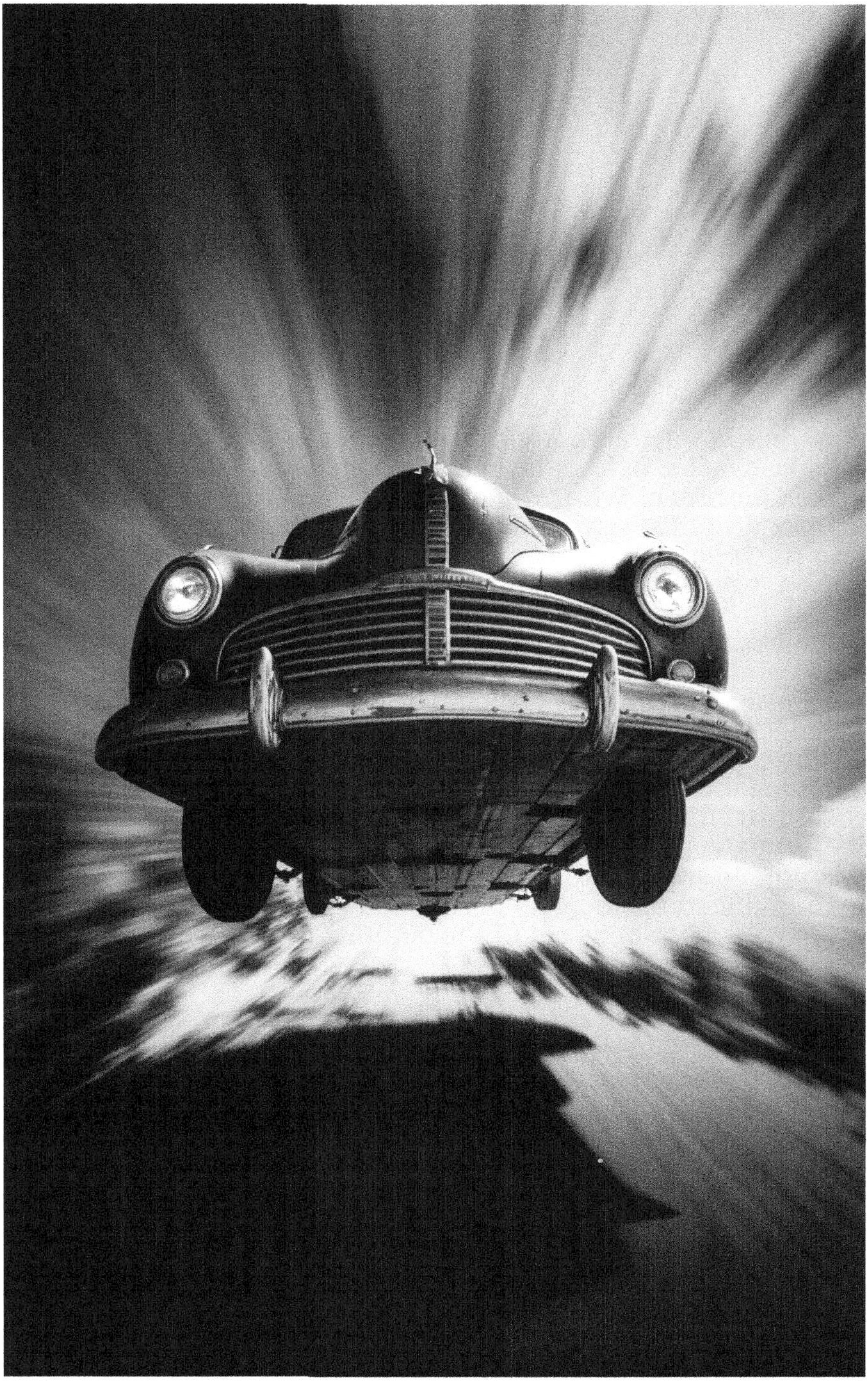

Chapter 6

When I'd shuffled that little bit to my left, I'd spotted a short but stout tree branch sticking out several feet below the edge, just visible before the light dropped away. As I fell, I tried to land on the branch with my feet, but my shoes slipped clean off the damp bark, and my stomach hit the branch winding me. I grabbed onto the branch and just managed to get a purchase on the side of the ragged quarry bank with my right foot to help support my weight. I was hanging just under the ridge and I heard the engine of my car purr into life. Next thing, I could hear the crunch of gravel, and the light overhead intensified. I was clinging there for dear life and I watched the underside of my beloved Ford pass over the edge right above me. I tucked my head into the bank to avoid getting clipped. I felt the rush of warm air as the car went over me, and it fell into the darkness. It was a San Quentin lifetime before I heard the distant, sickening sound of my Ford being mutilated on the quarry floor below. I was breathing hard, and I managed to hoist myself up onto the branch and got my shoes onto it. I used my burning stomach as a fulcrum and clambered over the edge just how Buddy climbs out of the bathtub; dishevelled, pride hurt, but still alive.

At this point I wasn't even thinking about the loon who'd pushed my car over the edge - getting out of the bottomless pit had been my first goal. I could see little but darkness and I slowly got to my feet and leant up the nearest tree to get my breath and rub my sore stomach which felt like a knife had been dragged across it. I staggered up to where the bicycle had been and stared down the narrow road. I could just make out a small pool of light about a hundred yards away, and knew it was Gun Happy heading back towards town to pick up his drive. I wanted to run after him, slug him, bring him back here and throw him over the edge to give him the treatment intended for yours truly. In my current state I could hardly walk, and then I started thinking... Pretty soon, anyone who had it in for me would think I was dead and gone. My car was sitting at the bottom of the quarry, and even if they couldn't find me, chances are I'd be down there somewhere, in little pieces.

I had to get back to the city, but that wasn't happening tonight. I made the most of the mild night and found a spot in the bracken, making my bed there. I did manage to sleep for a couple of hours, between waking, and imagined I was floating above the quarry looking down on the mangled wreck of my Ford, which was still lighting the floor of the pit with its headlights. Among the rocks and debris I saw pieces my body strewn about, like parts of a doll thrown in the trash by an ungrateful young girl. The image then slowly faded and I could hear a name being spoken lowly, over and over, echoing around the quarry.

"Jean Henry, Jean Henry, Jean Henry."

When the morning came, I was bruised and beaten, but still breathing. I made my way stiffly down the narrow road which seemed quite different in the daylight with birdsong and the warm breeze in the trees. Eventually I was back at the T junction, and I slowly made the trek back to Fable and went to the guesthouse again, watching my back and holding my stomach. Last night I could have been sleeping in a nice comfortable bed here, but instead I was lying in quarry ferns, with a cramped gut and damaged pride. I used the guesthouse phone to get me a cab back to Carnock, which would cost all the change I had and more, but I couldn't get there soon enough. After a long wait in a quiet room, the cab arrived and I was back in the city by mid-afternoon.

I got dropped at my apartment, made myself a bite and went over everything I knew so far. I strongly suspected that one or more of the residents of Cranborough were involved in the murder of Alessi, but I had no motive. I couldn't figure how the old French pistol came into play, but I suspected that little Marci Alessi was still alive, perhaps within Cranborough's sprawling walls. I needed to return to the estate, and after taking a bath and making myself human, I went out and rented the cheapest ride I could find, and that evening I went down to my office in town to check my messages. I had four. I was spoilt.

The first was from a woman who wanted me to catch her cheating husband. That'd have to wait. The next was from the tax office reminding me my bill was due. Last month. That would have to wait too. The third message was from Vince, who said he had some new information on the Alessi shooting. The last message was from Dorothy, the dame from the Museum. She said she was interested in my findings on the pistol robbery. This lady was definitely one gun crazy dame. Choices. I figured Vince was priority number one, and it sounded like Dorothy was more interested in getting leads than giving them. I couldn't return Vince's call as it was from a payphone, but I knew he'd be over the road in Diablo's this evening, where I went with Anna a few nights back. As for Anna, there was nothing from her but I wasn't about to visit her apartment again while I was dead. Going to Diablo's was hardly low-profile, but I knew Vince would be in the backroom playing poker, away from the public gaze. So later on I put my hired jalopy in the rented garage and went to the club on foot, via the alley at the back of the joint, rang the bell and asked for Vince. His cards round hadn't started and he was knocking back a beer at a small bar in the corner.

"Hiya Vince!"

"Good to see you Brix. Take a seat."

Vince got behind the little bar and offered me a drink. I painfully declined.

"I hear you have something for me Vince?"

"Yeah. I've got two leads for you. Firstly, Mark Alessi wasn't killed in view of the general public. The team found blood from the impact shot in a trailer at the back of the fairground, but little else in the way of prints, fibres and such. We had initial witnesses saying they'd seen Alessi get shot, but they must have seen him staggering through the crowd with a bullet in his skull and assumed they heard the shot. What with the shooting gallery as well..."

"So," I replied, "that's why no-one got a view of the killer, which was odd considering..."

"Yeah, the middle of a public space, and the firearm was discharged at close range. And there's something else. I was going through Alessi's criminal records with a fine toothcomb, and found a connection to Fable."

"Vince, that's fantastic. Shoot!"

Just then one of the card sharks came up to the bar and poured himself a stiff one.

"We're starting the game in five Vince."

"Ok Sam."

Vince took a slow drag on his smoke, and when Sam had taken his seat back at the table he continued.

"I went right through Alessi's records. He had a juvenile caution for disruption of the peace and being drunk and disorderly in the town of Fable, along with three other youths back in July 1920. Make of that what you will."

"Good work Vince. So, Alessi was in Fable back in '20. Oh, I should tell you I'm officially dead, my car and my body are somewhere at the bottom of the quarry just outside Fable. So it's best that I stay dead for now, if you catch my drift."

"I do. So how did you buy it?"

Just then the little stout card shark piped up;

"Vincent! Get your ass down here! We got a game to play. You in or out?"

Vince was in. And I was out the door. I knew I owed Vince and his missus a nice Christmas present this year. The guy was the best. I really couldn't do what I did without Vince Fury, as he was known by close ones.

I got back to my rental, and started on the road back to Fable. The light was fading, but the light bulb filament in my head was fizzing. I was still aching like blazes, but had to put that at the back of my mind. I had to go and get me the girl.

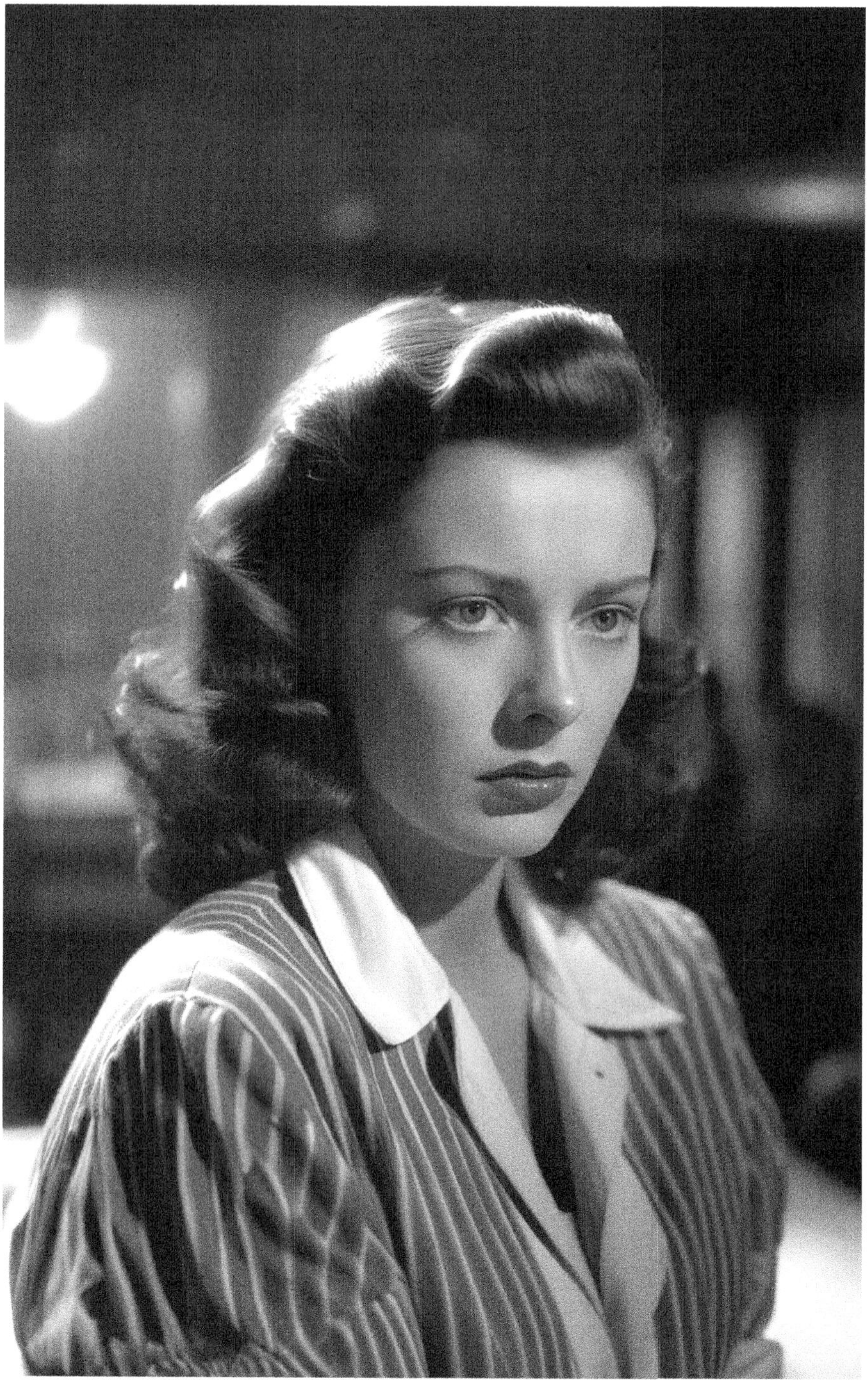

Chapter 7

By the time my tin can rolled into Fable it was night. The sky was clear and the lack of city light and fumes gave me a rare view into the cosmos, with no high buildings save the corn store tower just off the main drag.

This time I didn't drive into town central but veered off up a track which I'd seen last time, which led into a thicket of woods. I left my heap in the trees, out of sight, and made my way on foot. I had nothing but my gun, flashlight, my smokes and some bennies - for if I wasn't sharp enough. I skirted around the edge of the sleepy town until Cranborough was in sight up on the dark hill, a few of its windows orange lit. It wasn't long before I reached the base of the hill where I'd been before. This time I thought I'd check the outbuilding, and I slunk through the starlit night, and sidled up to a stout old tree on the left side of the small building.

The lights were out and there was no sign of life. I approached and had a peek through the side window. There was a gap in the curtains but all I could see was darkness. I was just about to explore further, when suddenly the light came on inside so I rushed back to the tree. Through the small gap in the curtains the light was sometimes broken as someone moved around inside. A couple of minutes later, the light went off again. I waited several minutes and there was no light, no action. Where had they gone? Were they asleep? I tried the front door. Locked. I got down low and swept my little flashlight across the ground. There were a couple of rocks and flower pots in front of the building. I checked them for keys. Nothing. The occupant must have the key and they've locked the door from the inside. Could it be Marci?

I knew the door might be alarmed but I had to chance it. I forced it, and being an old, weathered piece of timber it gave in surprisingly easy. My flashlight swept across the room and found no doors and no bed. This didn't make too much sense. There was a table lamp so I put it on the floor and flicked the switch, which spread a glow around the room. Still no doors. How the hell could someone have been here? There was nothing obvious to see, no belongings, clothes, toys. Just basic furnishings, a small fireplace, and a chest of drawers - which I quickly scoured to find nothing but moth-bitten clothes. I walked over to the other side of the room towards a little trash can, to see if there was anything incriminating. As I did I tripped on a crease in the old rug beneath me, and nearly got a closer look in the trash than I wanted. Impulsively I picked up the rug and threw it aside.

There was a trapdoor in the floor. I tried it. There was no lock, just a catch. I lifted the door and lowered myself down onto the stone floor my light could see below, and I shut the trapdoor above me.

About twenty feet ahead, down a tight corridor there was a flight of stone steps leading up. I listened hard and could hear only silence. I got to the steps, killed my light and made my way up in the dark, with nothing but a cold, metal handrail to guide me. The steps then began to curl around upwards, and I guessed I was climbing the inside of the hill - with a thousand tons of hulking mansion above my head. The air was cold and damp, and I could already feel it getting to my chest. The stairs continued. I finally ran out of rail and my hand slipped off the edge of the metal, as my left foot went down hard on a step that wasn't there. My flashlight found me on a small, circular landing with rails above the staircase, and there was a door around the other side of the space. The door was solid metal and locked. But there was a keypad next to it numbered 0-9. Was this the end of my ascent, and now the only way down?

I put some light on the keypad, and noticed that three of the numbers were a little worn, a bit smeared. 2, 5 and 9. I figured these buttons had seen some action in their time. I tried "2, 5, 9" and the door was steady. "5, 9, 2", "2, 9, 5", "9, 2, 5" and bingo! I heard a click and slowly opened the heavy door, not knowing what the hell was going to greet me. But at least I was packing a loaded pistol, and the bennies I'd taken earlier were kicking in. I found myself in a small space with a short set of metal ladders on the wall leading up to a hatch. I pushed the hatch and it opened. I lifted myself up with a sense of dread apprehension into the room above, thinking I could be a sitting duck in the shooting gallery...

I was in a room that appeared to be a library, with big shelves loaded with big reads. I listened, and could hear nothing but the bookworms gnawing, and the low hum of the tube light above. There were two doors leading out of the library, and the first I tried was locked so I opened the second, which led into a corridor. At the end was another door, and there were two doors off the corridor on either side. I then heard creaking footsteps approaching, but I couldn't tell from where. The safest option might have been to go back but I was much closer to the left and right doors, so I took a heavy breath and tried the right hand door, which opened into a bedroom - thank God an empty bedroom. The room was lit only by moonlight which crept in through a small window. My flashlight guided me under the bed where I waited. As the footsteps got louder I killed the light and held my breath as the door opened, and someone entered.

The light came on, and I could see shiny, chocolate brown shoes on a small woman's feet, as they paced around. I thought of my narrow cliff escape from the thugs, my almost being swallowed by the quarry. And now, I was hiding under a bed from a small woman with delicate feet, buzzing from both bennies and natural adrenaline. The woman left and I finally took a deep breath of stagnant air. I rolled from under the bed and listened at the door. Nothing. I went back into the corridor and tried the door opposite. Locked. I headed for the door at the end of the corridor, which opened into a dark balcony landing overlooking a large living room. There were voices and people below me. I could see a brunette, and a large man. They were arguing, but their conversation was vague. The woman threw her arms in the air like she was saying "Screw this, I've had enough."

I could just make out a small set of keys hanging off the woman's hips. I was guessing this was Jean, the sister, and the big guy was her brother - who could be our killer. I needed those keys. Jean strutted away and headed up the stairs that led to the landing I was hiding on. I figured she might be going back to her boudoir so I got there first, and slid into my usual resting place on the floorboards under the bed. Sure enough, she followed, and I heard her puffing and cursing, and saw her kick off her shoes. The one shoe came off close to my face, and I'm sure I could make out my own vexed reflection in the shiny vinyl. I heard wardrobe doors opening, and then felt Jean crash onto the bed above me. She was weeping.

I waited until the sobbing stopped. I felt like I'd been there an hour before I crept out from my hiding place. The room was lit by a small table lamp in the corner, and the curtains were now shut tight. I kept low, and looked around, noticing the set of keys on the cabinet above me. I reached up and pocketed them. I slowly stood up and saw Jean asleep in her bed, the covers partly off her, showing her face and shoulder. There was a frown fixed on her brow, even as she slept. I reached for the handle and quietly opened the door and crept out into the corridor.

By now it must have been the middle of the night, but I hadn't looked at my watch for hours. Did it matter? I tried each of the three small keys in the opposite locked door, and none of them fit. I headed for the balcony area, and took a look downstairs but it was too dark to see anything much. I heard a couple of creaks on the stairs and froze for a moment. False alarm? I stayed low and unseen. Or so I thought. My next memory was a short, sharp pain in the back of my head, and I can't recall much else.

I came around and I was in the big living room downstairs with the balcony above me. I was tied to a chair and there was a man and woman standing looking at me, and my head was as sore as my stomach. The large man had a gun in his hand, aimed in my general direction. I could see my shooter on the table, by Jean, not where it needed to be, in my hands.

"Detective! So, you've come back from the dead to poke your nose around our home have you?"

"So it was you who got the meatheads onto me? All I want is the girl," I grunted.

"Who's this girl? I don't know what you're talking about mister. The law in this country says I can kill an intruder, and that's what I'm gonna do."

"No Johnny!" pleaded Jean. "No more. I can't take it anymore. Enough is enough."

I was struggling for angles but had none.

"I've good reason to believe a missing girl is here, and she's been kidnapped. By you two."

"Have you now?" snarled Johnny. And what makes you think that? We're a decent family."

"Your mistake was your murder weapon. If you kill me, they're still coming for you. I'm not the only one who knows about your scheme!" I exaggerated.

"The old French gun? Ah yes, it was a sweet touch."

"Johnny! Just let him go!" pleaded Jean.

"Hush sis! This man ain't gonna be breathing soon, so the least he deserves is to know the truth, before he's buried."

"No more killing!" cried Jean, as I winced at those last words from Johnny's fat lips. He was a hulk of a man, you could never imagine he was once a baby - he must have been born like that, 300 pounds and with a solid jaw.

"It's story time, detective..." said Johnny, and I was a captive audience...

"Back in the age of innocence, before the flappers and the speakeasies, we had another intrusion here. It was the middle of the night and me and my sis were just kids. We had our mother and father, and were the perfect family."

"We were never perfect!" mumbled Jean.

"No, but our little world was. We had this house, and the family, and now it's just a hollow shell...like our mother."

Johnny continued..."On that night back in 1920, we were all asleep in our beds when they came. Our father heard the windows smash, their voices, and he went downstairs to investigate. All he had on him was his cane. He saw the monsters, and one of them had his prize possession, his antique French pistol - stolen from his collection. My father said they were wearing these laughing clown masks and were whooping underneath them too, like maniacs. The one with the pistol came over to my father and whipped it across his head. He collapsed to the floor at the bottom of the stairs. By now me and my sis were both awake in our beds, shaking. I ran to the balcony and saw mother running towards father and falling down the staircase."

Jean was sobbing hard. Things were starting to make sense.

"I ran down and mother and father were at the foot of the stairs. Both out cold. My father died in bed three months later after a stroke, and my mother was crippled from her fall. These people destroyed our family."

Jean piped up between sobs, "For years we never knew who was to blame, the police suspected that a gang of youths they cautioned in town a couple of weeks before might be involved, but they could prove nothing. And they weren't too interested in helping us. We were broken and we couldn't get any justice. One day this year I was visiting the city. I went to the museum to look around, and I saw the gun. I knew it was my father's piece - we had pictures in a catalogue. It was very rare. I asked them where they'd got the gun. They told me it was from Mark Alessi, the gangster. Naturally I told my brother."

"So," added Johnny, "I arranged to get us the gun back, as we had no actual proof it was ours. I found out all about Alessi, he might have been secretive but by the time I finished I knew more about his life than he did. I knew he liked to take his daughter to the fair the same day each month. I knew he never carried a shooter when he did. He thought it was a dirty thing to do when he was with his little girl. I stalked him, I cornered him when he was alone and took him into a trailer at the back of the shooting gallery. He wouldn't name other names. He would take them to his grave he said. I told him that wouldn't be too long. I let him know why I was ending his life and plugged him with the very pistol he'd taken from my family when he and his filthy friends destroyed us. He got off easy, but it needed to be done. The piece of crap still managed stagger out into the crowd, with a bullet in his head."

"What about the girl, Marci?"

"The girl ran away, I don't know."

"Look," I pleaded, "Alessi deserved it. He really deserved it. I don't blame you Johnny. Just tell me where the girl is, and let me go. What do you need with her?"

"I don't believe you!" spat Johnny. "And I don't know anything about the girl. If you still believe that, well, you aren't gonna stay silent are you? You found your answers. It's time you took them to your grave."

Johnny lifted his revolver, and aimed it squarely at my head.

"Johnny! Don't do it!" screamed Jean.

I closed my eyes, hoping my descent to purgatory would be swift and over with soon. Wishful thinking of course. Johnny pulled the trigger back. I saw the flash.

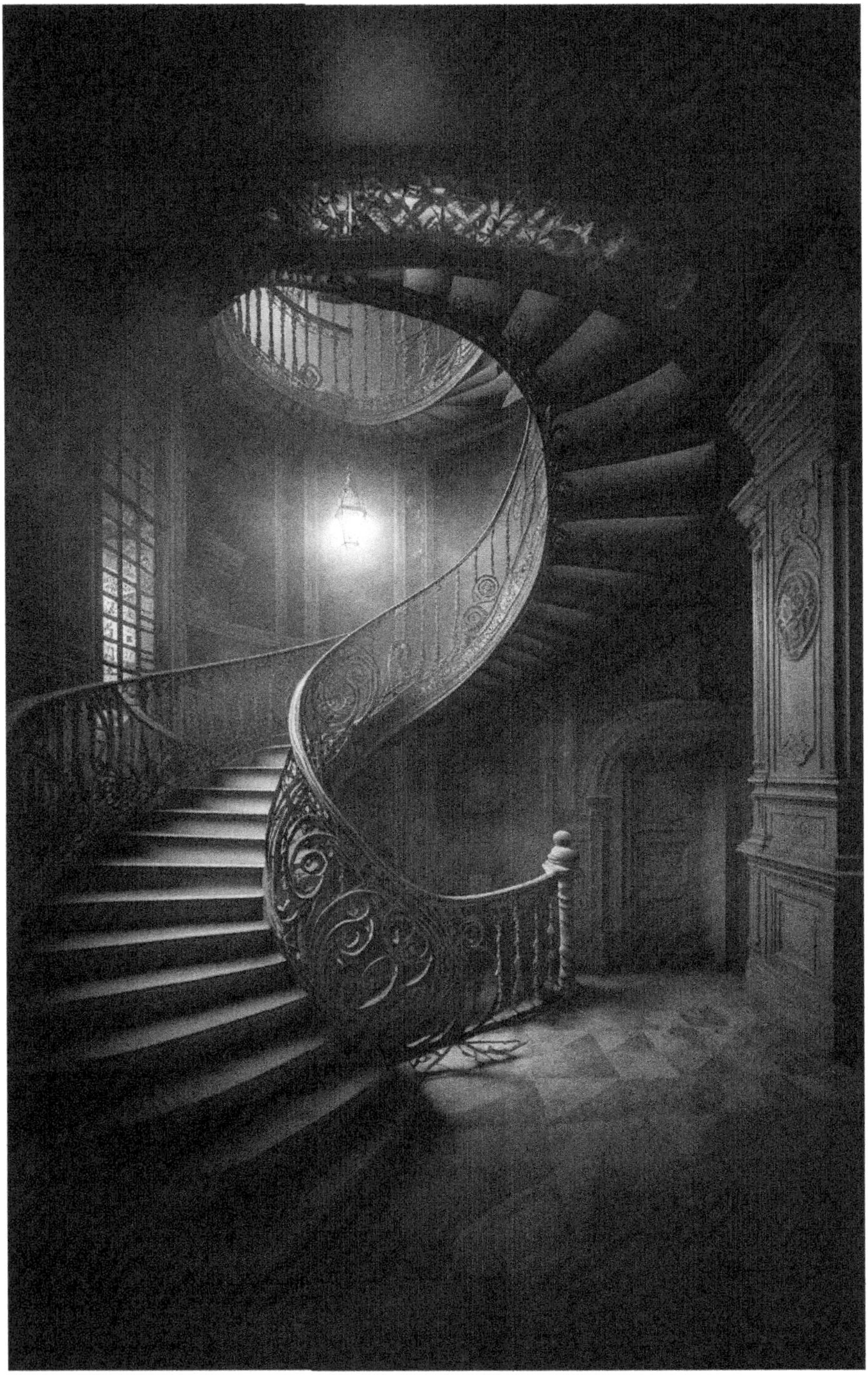

Chapter 8

Was I dead? I felt no pain, and my head felt light. All was dark, and I wasn't aware of anything - my senses and thoughts were gone. I then slowly realised I could still move my eyes around in my head and feel parts of my body. I flexed my arms, then my legs. Yes, they were still there. I slowly opened my eyes, and from blurred vision, I finally got my focus back to see the sorry picture before me:

Johnny was slumped on the floor in front of me, his neck snapped back by the force of his head hitting the ground, his left wrist also bent up on the floor, his revolver held loosely in his lifeless right hand. Just next to him was Jean, kneeling on the floor, her head in her hands, sobbing, my pistol on the floor in front of her. This must have been the gun that killed Johnny. My head was still ringing from being hit earlier, and my ears could still hear the echo of the blast. Jean finally looked up, her face all messed up and streaming with saltwater.

"I had to do it. I couldn't let him kill you."

"I owe you Jean. Can you loosen these ropes?"

I fell down on the sofa, and looked at the big, broken corpse spread over the floor in front of us. I didn't like the fact it was one of my bullets lodged somewhere in his back. Jean was still crying uncontrollably. I suddenly remembered we weren't the only ones in the house.

"Where's your mother Jean? And the helping hand?"

"She's in bed in the west wing, as she's been since your last visit. It's normal though detective. Hal is on duty tomorrow morning."

"I need some answers Jean. Is Marci here? In the house? I'm going to have to call the cops if your brother's to have a proper burial."

Jean placed a blanket over Johnny. The gun in his hand was evidence of justifiable homicide. But Jean had other potential charges

THE CASE OF THE MISSING DOLL   49

looming, and I hadn't even found the girl yet. Jean handed me the set of keys from earlier.

"Go and find her," she said.

"Well, tell me where she is and I'll get her, and then I need to deal with this. Then you can tell me just what the hell you planned on doing with her?"

Jean led me down a corridor which came to a winding staircase which curled around to the upper floor of the house. The old wooden steps creaked underfoot, and though the light was spare, I could just make out the stern faces of some of her ancestors who hung on the walls as we went up. At the top was a short landing and Jean unlocked a door and went in. I heard her talking, and then she asked me to follow. Marci was sitting on her bed, dressed in a pinafore with ribbons in her hair. She was the miniature, innocent version of her mother, like they were a pair of Russian nesting dolls. She looked up at me with sad, saucer-like eyes.

"Take me home mister," she begged me.

I sat next to her. "It'll all work out see. I'm going to take you straight back where you belong."

"I don't want her caught up in this circus Jean," I whispered. "I'm taking her back to Carnock City, and I expect you to stay here and wait for the cops, you need to put them in the picture."

"We'll be back shortly lovely," Jean reassured the girl.

I left the room with Jean and she led me into the room next door.

"So why did you do it, Jean? Why take the girl?"

"My brother was responsible. I couldn't stop him without reporting him, and believe me detective, I feared my brother. Johnny had been watching Alessi since I found the pistol in the museum. He was obsessed, and no-one understands more than me why he was so determined to get revenge for all that's happened since that devil set foot in our home. But I had no part in the plan - I found the pistol in the museum, that's all. We've been good to the girl, and she's become like one of the family."

"Seriously?" I scoffed. "You aren't her family! Poor girl must have been petrified! And I know you were involved Jean, more than you say you were."

"She spent most of her time with nannies and minders - hardly saw her father, let alone her mother. That's what the girl says."

"What the hell were you going to do with her, keep her locked up here forever like Mary Queen of Scots?"

"Johnny was going to take her to Mexico with his girlfriend and disappear."

"And this girlfriend? She was going along with it?" I asked, not really buying it. "I think your brother was going to kill Marci, just like he was going to kill me."

"No! No, he wouldn't have done that!"

"Come on Jean, we're calling the cops, there's some cleaning up to do downstairs and it's not gonna be me that does it. I'm taking the girl back to the city, and it'll be dawn by the time I get there. That was my job. The cops can deal with the rest of this mess now."

Back downstairs I rang police headquarters, told them to come find a corpse, then I hung up before they could ask me to hang around. I took Marci back to my flivver in the woods, and drove back to Carnock. She sat in the back clutching her doll. I felt bad for her. Her father was a hoodlum who'd taken her away from her mother. Then another hoodlum had taken her away from her father, permanently, and locked her away in a strange house. All I could do was tell the kid that everything was going to be alright.

"Will I see mom?" she asked nervously.

"Sure doll, you will. She asked me to come and get you."

Through the rear view mirror I saw a little smile form on her lips, and then the corners of her mouth turned down.

"I hated it there."

"Well you won't be going back. Try not to worry, it's all over now."

Marci closed her eyes and hugged her doll close to her chest, like she was praying with it.

"What's her name?" I asked.

"Shirley," she mumbled.

"Do you always look after her and make sure she's safe?"

She nodded her head vigorously.

"Have you ever lost Shirley?"

"Yes," she said. "I left her at the station once and she was put in the lost things."

"But you got her back?"

Marci nodded slowly.

"Well you've been lost, and your mom is now going to get you back," I reassured her.

Night turned quickly into day on the drive to the city. Marci fell asleep, and I watched the sun get higher as the suburbs drew closer. I was fizzing with the thought of reuniting Anna with her daughter, hopefully for good this time. I made my way across town, and then towards Anna's leafy neighbourhood in the valley. I parked up near her block and called her apartment.

"Hello?"

Anna's silky tones were turned into crackles through the intercom speaker.

"Anna. It's me, Brix. I got someone for you."

"Who? What do you mean?"

"She's about four feet tall and not bad looking" I said, getting a shy smile from the girl.

The intercom went dead, and before I could draw another breath Anna came bursting out of the doors and Marci ran into her arms. They hugged each other for forever.

"Hey, you got one of those for me?" I asked.

Anna gave me a good squeeze. Maybe nearly dying three times had all been worth it.

"Thank you detective. Thank you so much! Come inside, Come inside!"

We went up into Anna's apartment and the dame was as high as a kite, without the faintest whiff of Mary Jane. I told her about Cranborough, about the robbery, the siblings, the vendetta, the whole caper. She seemed to be only half listening, asking her daughter how she was, if she was feeling ok. Anna had an energy I'd not seen before. Sure, when she first came into my office that day she was full of living flesh and blood, in the full blossom of life, but she was pining for her daughter and there was an emptiness inside of her. The life she projected was all for my benefit, to draw me in.

Now she had her kid back she was truly alive, as alive as anyone I'd ever seen. As alive as someone who thought they were dying but then realised that they were a hypochondriac, and every living moment was a miracle to be savoured. Like someone who had a religious awakening, won the lottery and gave it all to the poor. It was moments like this that made my existence worthwhile. Even Anna's apartment seemed brighter than it had been before. There was less clutter on the table and even the walls. I guess she'd hardly care for her apartment if she didn't have faith that her little girl would return.

This wasn't over though. I had a court appearance to make as a witness in the trial of Miss Jean Henry.

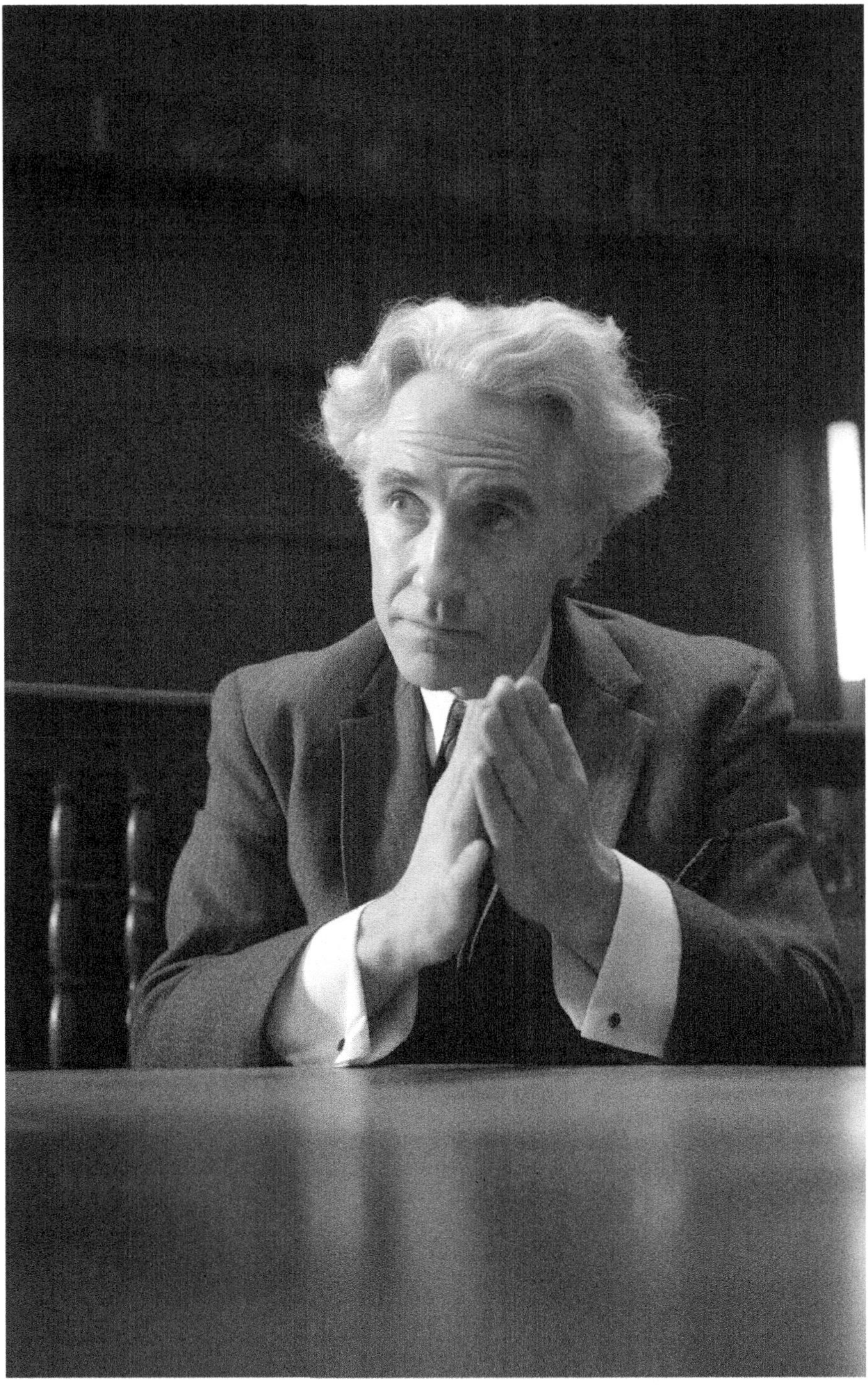

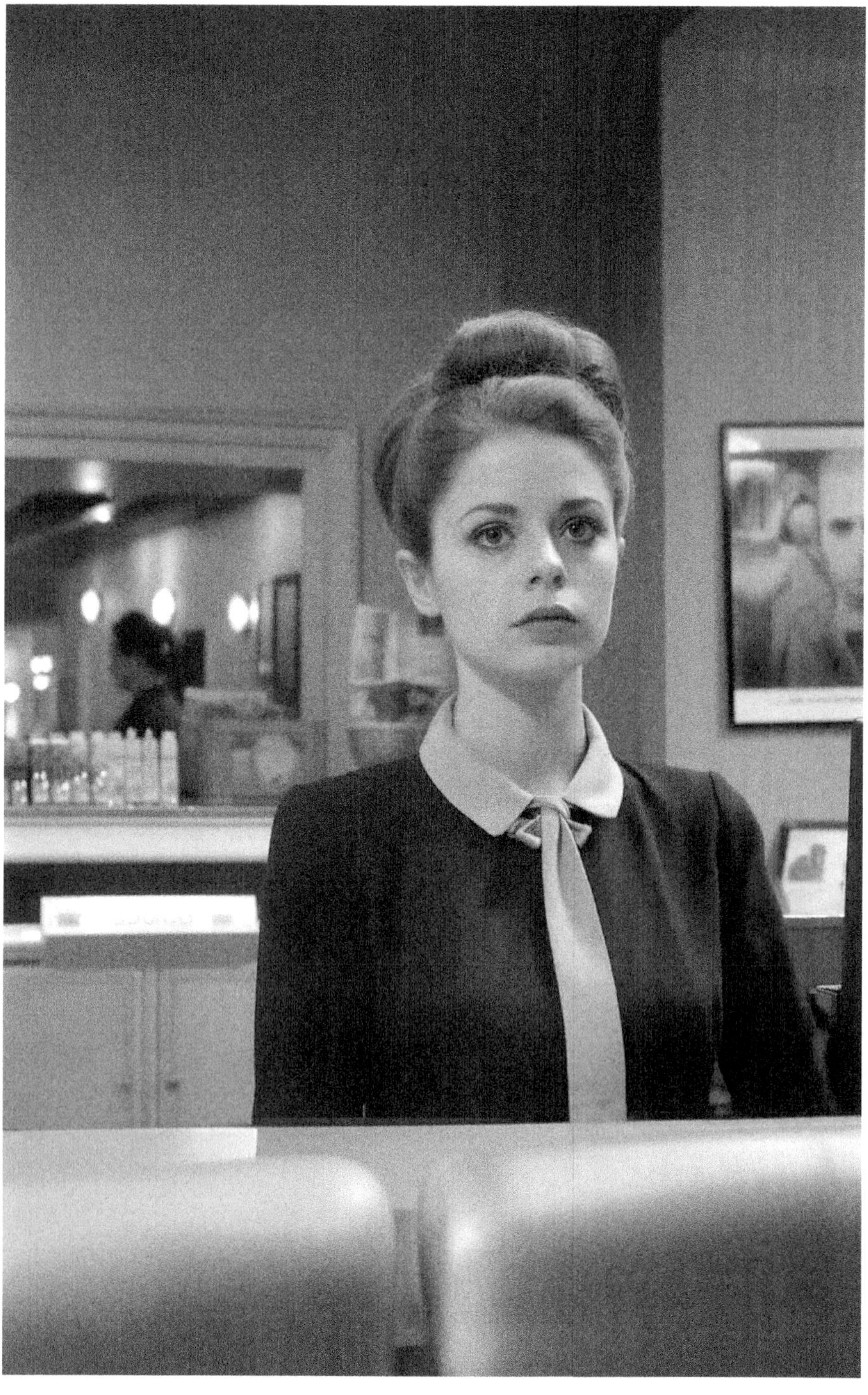

Chapter 9

It was a midweek morning in Carnock Central Court, and the room was filling up fast. The jury were already in place - twelve good citizens from various professions and backgrounds, all looking very serious, as I guess they should with such an undertaking. The accused was sat there with her defence lawyer, and the other side were still making notes and whispering to each other as folk spilled in through the foyet, many hearing about the case of "THE CRANBOROUGH MANSION SLAYING" in the Carnock Chronicle. The judge, Victor Benyak was sat on his throne, a spidery hand on his long chin, reading over notes, occasionally being interrupted by one of the lawyers or officials. There was a low hum of voices, the sweeping of footwear on the hard floor, and finally everyone settled down.

The judge made his presentation of the case against Jean Henry. Of course I wasn't there just on the part of curiosity. I was also a witness and had to relive the events of that night in Fable in front of total strangers.

Some familiar faces in the assembly included Dorothy and her colleague Harold, who I'd spoken to about the French pistol used in the Alessi murder. A few more people looked vaguely familiar, but there was no Anna.

Judge Benyak addressed the court: "Ladies and gentleman of the jury, I trust you will listen to all evidence, and carefully consider all that you hear. You will do so without prejudice, and make your conclusions without pressure and with clear minds."

I felt for Jean. Her fate rested on twelve random strangers, I hoped it wouldn't be her last supper. I wanted her to get off with saving my life, not a crime in my book. I couldn't forgive the pain she'd put that girl through by not standing up to her brother, and by protecting him - but I guess she'd lost her father, and I suppose her mother. Now she'd lost her brother too. I was sympathetic to the woman, but I was quite sure Anna would have a different take. As I thought about Anna, she entered the room, a silhouette in a blaze of sunlight which spilled in through the door, yet unmistakably her. She made her way to a seat near the back. The dame could even make the most of a courtly suit. She looked sensational but I put my little hankerings away for the serious business at hand.

Jean's lawyer was a sought after pro from up state who'd been around for years. He'd defended the innocent and the indefensible - from the wrongly accused, to gangsters of the underworld, and ordinary people who'd taken the law into their own hands. James Stern knew everyone had the right to a defence, and every defence lawyer needed to serve the judicial process. He was a wiry man of about sixty, with thick, wavy white hair. He looked a lot like an artist, and had flair to his movement somewhat like a dancer, moving gracefully around his little part of the courtroom. I'd seen the guy in action before, he really was something else.

His nemesis today was Brandon Talman, a short, stout, middle aged man, with broad features and a shifty kind of look. He was the kind of man you'd expect to be up in the dock not serving the court, if you held prejudices. Less experienced than Stern, he still had a reputation for playing hardball and never letting a case go until the fat lady was dead and buried. He had a young clerk with him, a nervous-looking kid with a crane-like neck and uneven teeth, probably teased at school.

The judge introduced the attorneys, and both Stern and Talman gave opening statements to the court, describing aspects of the case. Then Benyak spoke again:

"The charges brought against Miss Jean Henry are as follows:

Charge One: Being an accessory to the unlawful killing of Mr Mark Alessi.

Charge Two: Being an accessory in the abduction of a minor - Miss Marci Alessi.

Charge Three: The unlawful murder of Mr John Henry - brother of the accused."

I realised that didn't sound too good for Jean. When he'd finished with his grim formalities, and introduced the players, it was the turn of the prosecution and defence lawyers to dig out their experts and witnesses.

First off they had guys from ballistics and crime scene investigation give their opinions on the Alessi murder at the fairground, with experts showing the infamous Gallic gun to the jury, and describing every last detail of the murder scene. In my co-operations with the police bureau, I'd given them the murder weapon, which was found in Cranborough, and I'd had to explain how I got my lead about the estate. I knew the cops would ask the museum staff questions, so I didn't hide the fact that Jean was the person to ask about the pistol's origins earlier in the year.

The first few witnesses took the stand. These included a carny from the night of the Alessi murder who I don't recall, and a few revellers from that evening. There was no Madam Future, in fact there was no-one to corroborate first hand that Jean was there at all. That was good news for Jean. Just then, Harold, the museum curator took his oath. Prosecutor Talman questioned him.

"Mr McGuire, I understand that the weapon used in the Mark Alessi murder was originally a display item in your museum, donated by Mark Alessi himself several years ago. Is this correct?"

"Yes Mr Talman, that's correct."

"I also understand from your account made to the police that the murder weapon was enquired about by Miss Jean Henry sometime around February this year, is that also correct Mr McGuire?"

"Yes, it was Miss Henry who asked about the weapon's donor."

"And can you confirm that in early May of this year, the pistol was stolen from the museum where you are gainfully employed?"

"Indeed. We don't have any more information on this, except we think it was an inside job and a security man may have been involved."

"And why was this not divulged to the local police at the time?"

"Well, we didn't want to make a fuss about the robbery for the sake of the museum's reputation. Of course we didn't know for what purpose the pistol would be used."

"Thank you Mr McGuire, that is all," finished Talman.

When it was finally Jean's turn to respond to questions from the two lawyers, she knew that there was no evidence at present putting her at the Alessi murder scene, but she couldn't deny that she'd found the murder weapon, before it was used in the slaying.

"Miss Henry, were you aware of your brother's plans to murder Mark Alessi?" asked Stern.

"Mr Stern, I didn't know that my brother was actually going to go through with his mad scheme. He told me he was going to kill Alessi, that's true. I thought this to be mere rhetoric. I believed on the night of the murder that my brother was visiting a girlfriend in the city, I wasn't aware of his specific plans, nor did I assist them in anyway."

"So were you not present at Penumbra Park on the night of the murder Miss Henry?"

"I was not. I was at home with my mother."

"In fact," replied Stern "there is not a shred of evidence that you were at the scene of the crime is there Miss Henry? You're a woman of good character, with no convictions, a care giver to your mother. You're an artist who displays her work in Carnock, and you also sell your work to benefit the charities of the homeless. Is that true?"

"Yes Mr Stern."

"You're a devoutly Christian woman, who attends services at your private estate. Is it true you had suffered both emotional and physical abuse from your brother on past occasions?"

"Objection, Your Honour!" pleaded Talman.

"Sustained! Enough with irrelevant details Stern!" barked Benyak. "The jury will ignore the personal character assessment!"

When it was Talman's turn, he turned the heat up. To eleven.

"Is it not a fact that there are no witnesses to confirm you were at home that night Miss Henry? And that your mother, with whom you live could not corroborate your alibi?"

"My mother is not of sound mind and is ill!" spat Jean. "Is there, Mr Talman, a shred of evidence that I was with my brother? There is not, because I was not!"

"But you started the whole grim affair, didn't you Miss Henry? It was you who first found the murder weapon, the antique pistol, on display at Carnock Museum - as a previous witness, Mr McGuire has attested. And may I suggest that from that moment the fate of Mark Alessi was signed and sealed?"

"Of course I told my brother about the gun! It was a treasured piece of my father's, and when I discovered Mark Alessi was the donor I knew without a shadow of a doubt that he was involved in the robbery and murder of my father, because that's what it was...murder! They destroyed our family."

"Well, there you have it Miss Henry, deep grudges. The motive is crystal clear. Do you also think anyone can believe that your brother, Mr Henry was able to commit a cold-blooded murder in a public place and then take the victim's daughter away alone and unseen? Miss Alessi is too young to take the stand and is still in shock, but if that child could stand here today, she would tell a very different story - that she was tempted away from her father, and whisked away while her father was brutally slain!"

The infuriated judge broke in before Stern had the chance.

"Mr Talman! Do not make assumptions on what a person would recollect under oath when that person is not even a formal witness!"

When Talman had reduced Jean to an emotional wreck, it was my turn to take the stand, and speak of the events that lead me to Fable, firstly to Stern.

"Mr Mitchell, are you able to give a full account of your involvement in this particular case?"

"Yes sir, I am."

"Would you please describe how you came to be involved in the events in question?"

"Yes Mr Stern. Two days after the murder of Mr Alessi my services were enlisted to track down the missing girl, Marci Alessi."

As I spoke I glanced up at Anna, but she was looking at Jean, and I couldn't read her, especially as she was wearing shades.

"Please go on Mr Mitchell."

"So, the next day I made my way to the scene of the crime to gather information and get a feel for the place."

I went on, describing how I'd done a lot of digging (not mentioning Vince of course, or for that matter Madam Future. I decided it was better to hold some cards close to my chest.) I described how my trail had led me to Carnock Museum and eventually to Fable. Stern let me describe the events in detail, but I caught the judge glancing up at the large wall clock a couple of times.

Stern continued, "The police investigation found no direct evidence of any involvement by Miss Jean Henry in the murder of Mark Alessi. Did your own detective work find any suspicion, let alone proof of Miss Henry's involvement in, or presence at the scene during the crime Mr Mitchell?"

"It did not sir."

I had no absolute proof of Jean's presence that night, and I really had no intention of sending her to the can.

"I understand," continued Stern, "that before the defendant's brother Mr John Henry died he gave you an account of the murder of Mark Alessi. Is this correct?"

"It is Mr Stern," I confirmed.

"And did Mr Henry mention the presence or involvement of his sister, Miss Jean Henry during this discussion Mr Mitchell?"

"No he did not. His account only made reference to himself and Mr Alessi."

"Thank you, Mr Mitchell. No more questions your honour."

When it was Talman's turn, he threw questions at me like unpinned hand grenades.

"Mr Mitchell, may I ask where you obtained information regarding the French pistol that was used in the murder of Mr Alessi at the fairground? This detail had not been divulged to the press?"

"I have my contacts, but I never divulge my sources Mr Talman."

"I would suggest to the jury," said Talman, leaning on the banister and looking directly at the twelve, "that you are a man who thinks that flouting the laws of this country is of no concern. Obtaining evidence by illegal means and breaking and entering - as will soon be divulged."

"Objection, Your Honour!" Stern was rattled.

"Sustained!" said Benyak. "The witness is not the person on trial today Mr Talman. Please abstain from misdirecting the court from its purpose."

"Apologies, Your Honour," lied Talman, having made his point that I was a no-good, dirty, private dick who'd throw his own grandmother under a speeding train for a jukebox nickel.

The case dragged on for much of the afternoon, after which I headed back to my apartment. I had an unusually good night's shuteye aided by a sleep pill courtesy of a doc buddy, and the court reconvened the next morning. The second day the main topic of discussion was the killing of John Henry, brother of Jean, at the family mansion. The police experts were out again, describing the scene of the crime and their findings and opinions. Of course this time the only living witnesses were Jean and myself. Again, Jean's man Stern was first to ask questions.

"Miss Henry, can you tell us the events of the night in question, the night that your brother died?"

Jean sniffled, and her lower lip trembled, but she eventually managed to find her voice.

"My brother and I...we'd been arguing. I couldn't stand seeing the girl cooped up anymore in the house. I thought she should be back with people who loved her."

"You didn't think it your civic duty to call the police and report your brother for what he had done Miss Henry, and return the girl to a relative or guardian?"

"You don't know...didn't know my brother Mr Stern. He was not someone to be...contradicted. I wanted him to see sense, but he wouldn't. He thought he was starting to build up a rapport with Marci. I heard him telling her how wicked her father was, and how he'd "rescued" her. But how could he release her when she could identify him, and the house? I think he just thought he could keep her there forever, a captive witness."

"And you were trying to make him see sense; that this couldn't continue?"

"Yes sir. But then things got worse. Mr Mitchell turned up unexpectedly, and was assaulted by my brother.

Johnny then bound him to a chair and took his gun. I knew for certain that Johnny was going to shoot the detective; after all he'd already killed once. So I begged him to stop."

"You pleaded with him to let the detective go?"

"Yes, but then I heard him cock the trigger, and I had no choice but to save an innocent man."

"Thank you Miss Henry."

Brandon Talman ripped into Jean for the second time.

"Miss Henry, you say that you could not report your brother. He had this hold over you. Surely if you had reported what was going on, it would have put you in a better position now, but you didn't. I think you were fully involved in the whole plan."

"Please", piped up the judge "stick to the charge we're currently on, the death of John Henry at the Cranborough house. And "thinking" is not enough Mr Talman."

"Apologies, Your Honour," answered Talman, clearly angry with himself. "Miss Henry, you say that your brother was going to kill Mr Mitchell, and you had no choice. No choice at all, is that right?"

"Yes Mr Talman, that's right."

"In fact, it was actually very unlikely that Mr Henry was going to take the life of Mr Mitchell at that moment, and I think you knew this full well."

"I don't know what you mean, that's ridiculous!" answered Jean, frowning hard.

Talman turned to the judge. "We have a piece of evidence from the night, which we thought would best be served when interviewing the defendant. Can I please bring back the ballistics expert your honour?"

Jean looked as bemused as I was. The ammo guy stood up and spilled:

"The gun found in the hand of Mr John Henry that night contained only blank rounds your honour."

There was a loud intake of breath in the room, and then muttering grew louder.

"Silence in court!" demanded the judge.

My God, this was an astonishing turn in the case. So, I'd never been in danger of certain death? But I couldn't figure why the hell Johnny would be packing dummy slugs.

"I...I had no idea Mr Talman, I don't, I didn't know the gun had blanks. Why would the gun have blanks?" stuttered Jean.

"I put this to you Miss Henry. Earlier on you swapped John Henry's live rounds with blanks, and then later on you took his life in cold, calculated murder. This was not an act of mercy, but an act of cold-blooded evil."

"I did it to save the detective!" cried Jean. "I don't know anything about blanks! Nothing at all!"

It was soon my turn to take the stand again and be questioned by James Stern.

"Your detective work bought you back to Cranborough for a second time, is that correct Mr Mitchell?"

"Yes, I made a covert entry of the property..."

Talman made a little wry smirk.

"My objective was to find Marci Alessi."

"Because you were confident at that time that Miss Alessi was in the building?"

"Yes. I knew the girl's life was at stake and I was unlikely to obtain a warrant through legal means at the time. So, I entered the property via an outbuilding and I found a hidden entry point into the main house."

I went on to describe my strange predicament under Jean's bed, leaving the room, observing the heated exchange downstairs, and what followed...

"The next thing I know, I'm tied to a chair with a gun pointed at my head by Mr Henry. I was unarmed, and Jean was begging him to leave me alone. She was pleading with her brother, pleading for him to stop threatening me with my life."

"In your opinion Mr Mitchell, was Jean in fear of her brother? Did you get the impression that he was dominating and controlling her?"

"Objection!" blurted Talman.

"Sustained! Rhetorical questions, please keep questions open Mr Stern!" Benyak fumed.

"Withdrawn. What happened next, Mr Mitchell?"

"John Henry made it crystal clear of his intentions to silence me Mr Stern. I'm quite sure he wanted to put me in a shallow grave. But before this he gave me an account of his involvement in the murder of Mark Alessi, details I furnished the police with and which Jean Henry has corroborated. He then aimed at my head, and the next thing I was aware of, Jean was on the floor sobbing, next to her dead brother. She was of course traumatised by what she'd done, and she covered her brother with a blanket. She would have stayed with him, but I made her show me where the girl was."

"In your opinion were Miss Henry's motives for her actions on that night in any way selfish or predetermined Mr Mitchell?" asked Stern.

"Mr Henry's death was not predetermined in my opinion as an observer, and was a selfless act in my defence by the accused, Miss Jean Henry."

As I spoke, I saw Anna turn her face towards me. With her shades on, and just the vaguest hint of her eyes it was impossible to know her true expression, but I imagined she was pretty sore for my defence of Jean, who'd been complicit in her daughter's captivity at the house, and God knows what else...

"It is now the turn of Mr Talman. Please proceed," said the judge.

"Mr Mitchell, you suggested earlier that Miss Henry saved your life, is that correct?" asked Talman.

"Yes. Until the blanks. I was sure she'd saved my life."

"I would therefore claim that your favourable view of Miss Henry is in direct relation to your gratitude to her."

"Not at all. I have no doubt, from first-hand experience that Miss Henry acted on my behalf, to prevent my demise."

"No bias at all then?" Talman said sarcastically. "No further questions, your honour."

The jury, went out to deliberate. I breathed a sigh that this chapter was over. I headed out to the coffee shop around the corner to get myself a cup of mud. The city folk went about their business oblivious to the knife-edge drama that overlooked them. I thought about what a labyrinth of a case this was. I'd felt for weeks that I was missing something, there was some wood I couldn't make out for those damn trees. I knew there had to be more to this business. If Johnny thought nothing of taking my life, then why did he spare Marci and keep her locked away in Cranborough? And Jean... just how scared of her brother was she? Was this just a ruse? If she'd been involved in the kidnapping then either she was fully complicit, or her brother must have had a strong hold over her. I sat there sipping my coffee, as a familiar face smiled in my direction. It was Dorothy.

"Well, Dorothy, How are you?"

"I'm fine Mr Mitchell, mind if I join you?"

"Please do. Call me Brix, I've had all I can take of Mr Mitchell for one day."

Dorothy smiled, took a seat and ordered an espresso.

"Badly needed," she noted, taking it down like a shot of rye. "I don't think I've properly introduced myself have I? The name is Dorothy Taub."

She offered the dainty fingers of a black-gloved hand, which I duly squeezed.

"Interesting case, Dorothy. I've done my bit. I hope Jean gets a break. She seemed like the real deal to me, when I had that gun in my face. If she knew the gun had blanks, she's a mighty fine actress. She should be up there on the silver screen, the new Bette Davis."

"Ida Lupino even!" enthused Dorothy. "But I think her brother was a beast! I mean, he nearly had two murders on his hands, at least one murder and one attempted murder."

"Yes, he seems as cold as the man he killed."

"I'm not sure if this mess has done the museum any good, but they say any publicity is good publicity."

"You'll be fine. I really feel I'm missing something though Dorothy," I admitted.

"Really, Brix?"

"Yes, I feel like the answers are staring me in the face. I found the Alessi killer - well the killer found me. I got the motive - well the killer gave me the motive. I found the girl - well Jean gave me the girl." I laughed. "I did have to be in the right place though, right?"

Dorothy smiled. "Yes. And the two guys, Stern and Talman, they paint very different pictures of Jean. Who is the real Jean I wonder?"

"But it's the girl that's playing on my mind. The girl and her balloon, there at the fairground in the fading light. She's now back in her mother's arms, but the image haunts my dreams Dorothy."

Dorothy and I talked more about the case. She was an intellectual gal, well read, learned. But not the kind that would tie a simple guy like me up in knots for kicks. She was earthy. My kind of dame. At least the kind of dame that was good for me. But there was something Dorothy said that rang strange bells in the back of my mind; "Pictures of Jean." I had no idea why.

The break was over. The two of us walked up the court steps through the open entrance doors, into the foyer. People were heading for the courtroom, and I found my seat in the house. The atmosphere was buzzing with static and alive with nerves. If Jean was found guilty of the third and final charge, she might not fry, but she'd be looking at a hefty sentence. I guessed there were no more Henry family members in that room, but I got the feeling that there was sympathy for the woman.

Everyone took their place, judge, jury, and the last few bodies scuttling into their seats. The judge played with his papers. The two attorneys fidgeted. Jean had her eyes closed. Was she praying? Anna had taken her shades off and was rubbing her eyes. People were on tenterhooks. Finally Benyak's voice boomed out:

"Members of the jury, have you made your verdicts?"

"We have your honour," replied the leading juror, an average-looking Joe, as jurors rightly should be.

"May I ask the elected member of the jury to please stand, and to give the jury's separate verdicts on the three counts?" requested the judge.

The head of the jury stood, and nervously read from his page:

"On the first count, being an accessory to the unlawful killing of Mr Mark Alessi, we find the defendant...

Not guilty."

"On the second count, being an accessory in the abduction of a minor, Miss Marci Alessi, we find the defendant..."

The pause seemed long. "Just give us the goddam verdict!" I thought. The tension in the room was palpable. Finally, Joe Average finished his sentence.

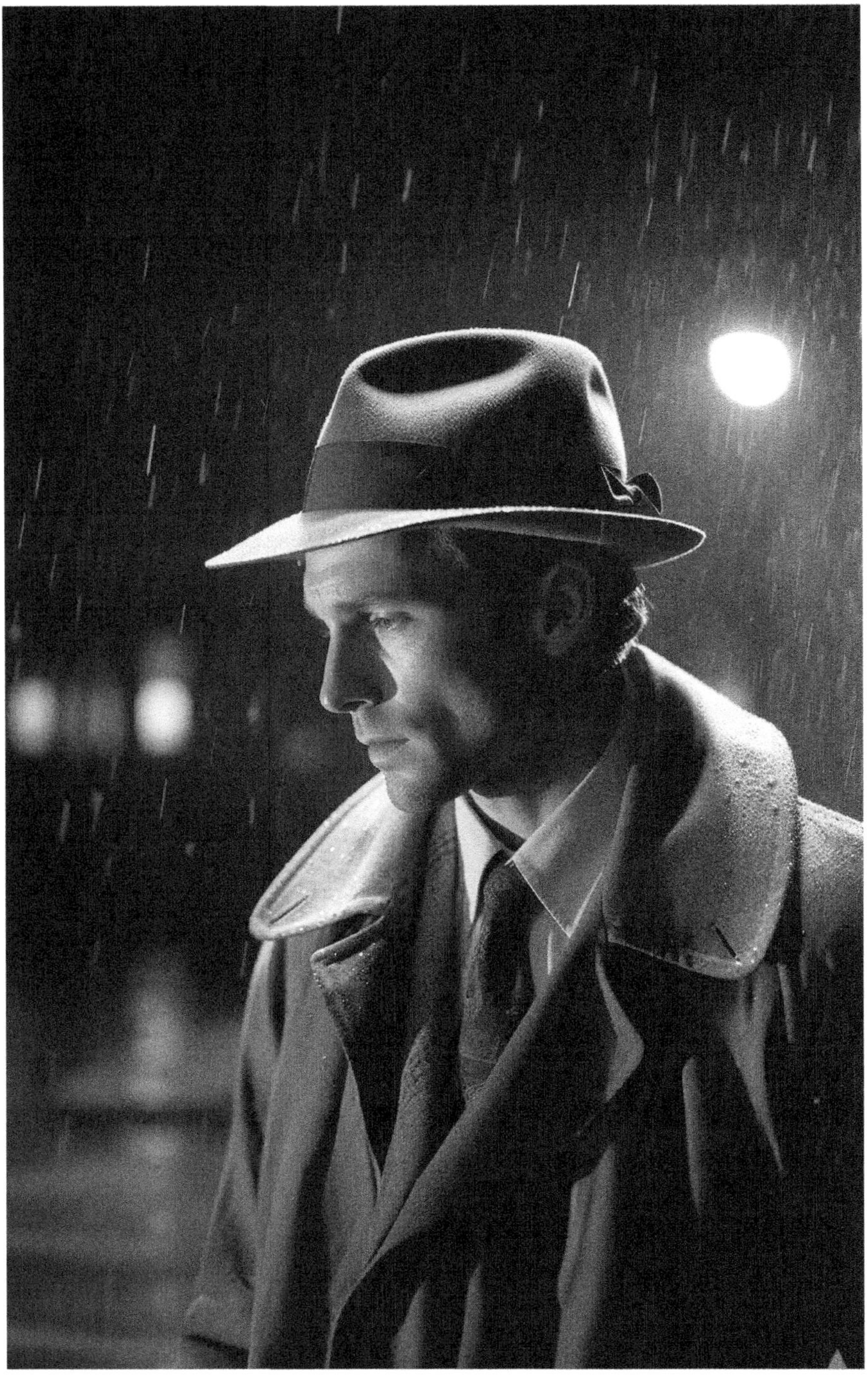

Chapter 10

The court was on a razor's edge as the jury made its second verdict of the three. I could see the fervour in every set of eyes as I looked around the room.

Finally, Joe Average spoke:

"On the second count, being an accessory in the abduction of a minor, we the jury find the defendant...

Not guilty."

Jean was visibly shaking.

"On the third count, the unlawful murder of Mr John Henry, we find the defendant...

Not guilty, Your Honour."

Jean's head dropped in relief as the tension seemed to dissolve from her body. I looked at Anna, she was sitting upright and her head fell slowly back like she was deep breathing. Stern shook his fist in the air and embraced Jean. Talman had his hands over his face and rubbed it. When he lowered his hands he had an expression of exasperation. People were talking loudly. I looked at Dorothy, and she returned the glance, lifting her eyebrows with a mock smile as if to say "Well, now we know. It's all over..."

But it wasn't, not quite.

"Quiet, please!" said Judge Benyak, who finally settled the court. "The jury has found Jean Henry not guilty on the three charges, but due to her concealment of crimes committed, that is the murder of Mark Alessi after the fact, and the active concealment of a child, I would normally sentence a felon to five years in state prison. In the case of Miss Henry, due to the circumstances and the death of her brother by her own hand in protecting Mr Mitchell, I will defer this sentence, and put Miss Henry on probation for a three-year period. Court is closed."

I made my way down to Jean, as the court room emptied, and gave her a squeeze.

"Thank you Mr Mitchell. Thank you so much."

I nodded, "Stay out of trouble Jean."

Dorothy made her way down and whispered in my ear, "Justice is served, I think. Stay in touch detective, you know where to find me." Her words tickled my ears like ostrich feathers. During all this, I saw Anna leave the building out of my peripheral. I wasn't sure what was going through her mind. She wouldn't have come to the court if she hadn't wanted to see a certain outcome. But she had her daughter back, and my job was done. A few nods were given and hands shaken, and then I made my way to the exit. I left the building down the stairs, behind the main flow of people leaving the court.

It was a twilight city that greeted me outside, and the moon was sat on a wisp of red cloud that trailed across an otherwise empty sky, like a wise old owl perched on a blood stained branch. The continual hum of daytime traffic was now broken bursts of engine sounds, and the odd siren and car horn. As the light was fading the illuminated shop windows were coming to life displaying their wares. The pedestrians were spilling in and out of bars and cafes, and the city seemed awake, but kind of calm.

I walked down the sidewalk past the street vendors and the newspaper stand which was empty of today's papers. It just had its pulp magazines; "Night Terrors", "Lust in the Sun", "Surprising Tales", with their lovingly sordid cover art. The empty spots were reserved for tomorrow's papers which were being typeset right now with the story of Jean's trial and would soon be zipping down hot presses for publication at dawn.

I was happy Jean got off, but I'd like to know how Anna had taken it. I guess she'd taken it badly. I'd see her again. I'd like to see the girl again too. As a private dick in the dark city, it doesn't pay to get sentimental but I had a soft spot for the Alessi girls. Yet my brain had an itch, I knew I'd missed something. The case wasn't done. There were still a few jigsaw pieces in my pocket, and I was running them through my fingers trying to make them fit. I knew Jean wasn't as innocent as she made out. I felt that Jean and her brother had been hiding something, other than the girl. After all, looking back at the afternoon I first went to Penumbra Park when I spoke to Madame Future, the old sage had seen Jean with Marci at the reading - she was an active accomplice. But I was glad no witnesses were there to send her down. The greater evil had been taken away that night.

***

It was a couple of months later, and the trial had faded from my mind. New cases had been coming in thick and fast with my courtroom appearance putting me in the public eye. Then one evening, after a day glued to my office chair going through letters, I went to a fancy Chinese restaurant I liked to eat at. I'd spent the evening enjoying the food and music and talking to a few regulars. I'd eaten my fill and headed out back in the direction of Diablo's to catch the breeze with my cop buddy in there. I continued down the sidewalk with not even my latest case on my mind. The wind picked up a little and I ducked into a doorway in the shadow of a street light to strike a match up for my smoke. Little did I know that the answers to my questions, the itch in my brain, were going to hit me like a sledgehammer in just a few seconds, merely because I'd stopped in that particular doorway.

I looked up at the sign over the window, and realised it was the city art museum and gallery, The Mocata. Its large window was lit by white light. I'd passed this window several times over the last month and not paid much attention - especially in the day when it wasn't lit up all nice. There were a few paintings displayed on stands and modernist sculptures. Not really my taste, but one particular painting caught my eye. It was a sensual portrait of a blonde woman, looking over her soft, bare shoulder. For a long moment I forgot to breathe. Those eyes were unforgettable.

They were Anna's.

It was Anna Alessi!

"Hell, what are the chances?" I thought. I then looked down at the small signature in the right-hand bottom corner of the painting. It was a signature I'd seen before. It was Jean Henry's. That's where I'd heard the name! Before I even went to the museum, before I spoke to Dorothy, and before I knew anything about the Henry family but a vague recollection of their name. The gallery must have put this painting in prominence due to Jean's trial, but they couldn't have known the significance of this particular portrait.

This meant that Anna already knew Jean, and Jean already knew Anna. She'd painted her, and there was a lot of emotion in that paintbrush. It then came to me where I'd seen the signature before. It was in Anna's apartment the first time I went; there'd been a painting on the wall signed by Jean Henry, among the others.

The next time I went to Anna's place the painting wasn't there and the wall looked emptier. I knew something was off but couldn't fathom it. Anna must have moved it, she needed to hide the fact she knew Jean. This was all like a firework in my mind, and it was all coming together. I thought again of Anna's apartment that first night. There was something else really odd. That white lipstick on the table. Damn, I'd been so dumb. It wasn't a lipstick. It was a tear stick. The type they use in the theatre, or cinema to get the waterworks flowing. Anna was crying crocodile tears. She must have known where Marci was all the time. But why?

I needed to know more, but I wasn't ready to go to her place before a drink. So I stopped off at my usual joint.

It was quiet in Diablo's, before the rush of the nocturnal crowd. I didn't seek out Vince in the back, I wanted some alone time. They had a pianist on, and the band would be up later. He was playing a Hoagy Carmichael tune, "Stardust." Hell, you can't go wrong with Stardust. I sat in a booth and a waitress came and bought me a drink, which I sank real quick. I put my elbows on the table and propped my head up with my hands. How could I have missed it? It was all there to see? But if Anna was in on the whole thing, then why the hell did she need me to find Marci? I couldn't sit here. I needed to know. I went to my garage, got my shiny new Ford, and made my way to Anna's apartment. It was late now. The sky was black, and the streetlights cast hard beams across the streets. I parked up and rang the number 12 bell.

"Hello?"

"It's me."

"Detective? It's kind of late...Let me get dressed. Give me five."

After ten, Anna let me in.

"Hope I didn't get you up?" I asked.

"No, it's fine. Marci is in the other room, asleep."

I took a seat and Anna offered me a drink.

"Rye, please."

"Here you go. What's it about, detective?"

"I'll cut to the chase Anna. The jig is up. I know that you knew Jean Henry. I know that you sat for her and that you were probably - are probably close with her."

Anna looked down and breathed out a long sigh, put her hands together over her mouth like she was praying and blew through her fingers.

"Ok, you're right. Is this going to go any further? I mean, to the authorities?"

"No. But I need to know Anna. You and Jean were in on this together, weren't you? Taking your daughter to Cranborough? And why the hell did you get me involved?"

"I'm not going to tell you anything else detective; unless you promise you'll not separate me and Marci again."

"Look, hell, I promise, Anna. But I thought you were real."

"Sometimes I was, detective..."

She flicked her lighter and lit a smoke. She offered me one so I took it. She continued.

"I knew Jean from visiting the gallery in town one day, maybe three years ago. I loved her paintings. I decided to go to one of her openings a few weeks later. We got talking and hit it off. I liked her, and she seemed to have this fascination with me. She'd led a sheltered life in the old house; home schooled, then helping care for her mother. Her art was her outlet to the outside world, a career I guess. And damn it she was good. I can't explain exactly but there's something about the way she uses the brush on the canvas. The way she layers the paint. I'd never seen anything like it."

Anna took a long, slow drag from her Marlborough, dropped some ash on her dress and flicked it off with long, lilac fingernails.

"We had drinks a couple of times in the city. Her interest in me seemed to grow. She asked if I could sit for her, so I went up to Cranborough and let her paint me. Think it was two February's back. The painting took a few days, so I stayed over there. Her mother put me up. It was before she went completely off her chump. The place blew my mind detective. It's quite the joint isn't it? Our friendship continued afterwards, and naturally I bought some of her work, this was before my split with Mark. Before the money started drying up. But she gave me the portrait after she'd copied it - one for herself and another variation for the gallery. I loved it, but thought it vain to put that one on my wall.

Then, the unthinkable happened. Mark left me and put the blame on me, saying I was an unfit mother. It was all fabrication - you can trust me on that. He had powerful lawyers in his pocket. He got custody. He loved Marci, but she was also like another possession of his. He didn't love her enough to let me see her other than occasionally. I spoke to her on the phone once or twice a week, if I was lucky, but it was killing me. Not too long afterwards Jean came to my apartment and told me she had some news that I'd want to hear.

Jean told me she'd found this antique pistol in the museum that belonged to her late father. She told me through her tears about the events of that night in Fable all those years ago, when the gang came and destroyed her family. She knew this was the only gun of its kind in the US. She said it was donated by my ex-husband. She and her brother now knew that Mark was involved in the robbery and assault. It made me hate him even more. I felt ashamed to have been with him. He was ruining my life, and he'd ruined their life. The man was far worse than I ever knew. How could I let him keep my daughter?

He'd told me I'd signed a clause written into the custody that if he died, Marci should be looked after by his aunt, who lives in Delaware. The next time I saw Jean, she told me that her brother Johnny was hell bent on killing Mark, but knew he couldn't get close to him. I told Jean that once a month, usually on the same day of the month, Mark took Marci to the fairground at Penumbra Park. It was his special time with her. He went there alone, no henchmen, no guns. It was one day a month where he pretended he was a normal human being."

At this point, Anna was sitting on a chair but she then moved over to the sofa, and laid herself down on it. She let her leg hang off the side, and put her hand through her hair. She looked at me, pursed her lips and frowned a little.

"I hope we can trust you detective? It's not just me, but it's my daughter who needs to know this."

"Carry on Anna, spill for God's sake."

"So, between us, we concocted a plan. I was due to have my catch up with Marci, that month, June. We agreed I could meet Mark at the fairground that evening. That was the hardest part of the whole plan. It took a lot of persuasion, but in the end the dope agreed; "This ain't gonna be no regular thing you know. It's only because it's her birthday this month, see?" he'd said to me.

I went to the fairground alone and met Mark there. I made sure I wasn't noticeable. I wore shaded glasses, had my hair tied back and covered with a hat. He didn't like that. "What's with the disguise?" he said. Little did he know. He loved my hair, but he didn't own me anymore."

Anna let out a wicked chuckle and took another drag of her cigarette before blowing a violent burst of smoke into the air.

"It's true; Jean wasn't there, that night. It was just me, Mark and Marci. And Johnny in the wings. The three of us were together like a family, for a few minutes at least. It pained me to see how happy Marci was in that moment. I told Mark I'd take her to the fortune teller. I knew Mark hated fortune tellers. When he was a kid one told him wherever he went death would follow. And the old crone wasn't wrong, huh? So we went to Madame Fortune, while Johnny took Mark at gunpoint to a trailer he'd hired under a false name at the back of the shooting gallery, where it was quiet and roped off. He tied Mark to a chair and gagged him. He gave him a sermon with every detail of how he'd ruined the lives of his family, and what an evil piece of filth he was, and left him there in the locked trailer to think it over. He then came over with the yellow balloon, which was the signal for me to wrap things up and leave.

I left with Marci and we headed up to where the car was parked. The yellow balloon was also so any witnesses would only remember the girl and the balloon, not the woman in dark clothing who was with her. It seemed to work didn't it? Madam Future had seen me of course, but I took the chance she wouldn't talk to the cops, or the cops wouldn't talk to her, as she was in her tent, away from the action. I kinda guessed you'd leave no stone unturned though. Anyways, Johnny went back to Mark in the trailer, but he'd managed to cut himself free and was waiting for Johnny behind the trailer door. When Johnny unlocked the door and went in, Mark tried to escape but Johnny pushed him back in. He pointed the gun at his head and gave one last short speech before finishing him. Johnny ran, and Mark managed to stagger out the door and into the public space by the shooting gallery, probably on account of him already having metalwork in his forehead from being kissed by a baseball bat.

Johnny escaped the commotion un-noticed and met up with me and Marci at the car over in the east side of the park, and we made for the ferry before the police arrived. Waiting for that ferry was hell. We couldn't time it too close, so were sat there waiting for, what, a quarter of an hour before the ferry came, and thank God they never stopped it. If the cops had seen me and Marci with Johnny we'd have been finished. Game up, detective."

"That was a big risk, that the cops would stop ferries in and out of there before you'd split," I said.

"Well the plan had been to leave the body in the locked trailer, to give us plenty of time to get away. Didn't quite pan out. But Johnny would have risked it anyways."

"Were you and Johnny...an item?"

"As far as he was concerned we were," she said. "In the few weeks I'd known him we'd gotten...friendly. He had this dream of us moving out to Mexico, somewhere in borderland, where the three of us could live as a happy little family."

As Anna made a little smirk again, I had to reflect. I knew Anna had the power to manipulate and hypnotise, but I was seriously losing track of just how many people she'd cast her spell on.

"Johnny took Marci to Cranbourough, and I told her that mom would see her soon. But I didn't want her there forever. I had to get her back to me. Permanently. So, I thought of you, Mr Mitchell."

"You did huh?"

"I knew your reputation for finding people and your discretion was second to none. I knew you'd been in the force and had your contacts. I knew you could bring my girl back home, where she belonged. And if you didn't, Mexico was always an option, I guess. I knew that neither Jean nor Johnny would know you'd been working for me, and I knew both of them would protect me, whatever the cost to themselves. And if they did want to drag me down with them where was the goddam proof I was involved? Maybe I should have known you were too sharp to ever fool you detective, and you'd find out in the end. But all that mattered to me was getting my daughter back, without any hint of my involvement. Nothing else. No one else."

"I think that's crystal," I replied, not really understanding how someone could be so heartless, but Anna did have a heart it was just...selective. Love makes you do crazy things and this love was as real as it gets.

"Was it the plan to kill Johnny, get him out of the picture?" I enquired.

"No, but I knew you'd be in danger, and once I knew you were on to Fable and the house, I knew I had to act. So when Johnny came round here the night before at my request, I put blanks in his gun. He wasn't in a habit of using it in general, but I had to protect you - after I knew he was on to you and had heavies involved."

"Heavies..." I scoffed. "I've had heavier."

"Johnny had come down here with Jean that night, but Jean stayed in the car down the street. Johnny asked me to come to Fable and stay there. I told him it was too soon, and not to come round again as the cops could be watching the place. I told him to give me more time, and I'd be up there in a couple of weeks if he could look after my baby in the meantime, and tell her she was safe. He said that was alright, he'd wait. But no longer than two weeks he said. I didn't want to go back there, to a place that could connect me to the murder of Mark and disappearance of Marci. I needed her here, with me, and you were the means detective. It wasn't in my plan for Jean to end up in court. I never wanted Jean to go down."

"Well, thank your lucky stars she didn't go down," I replied, "because if she'd found out you'd hired me, and her and Johnny were pawns in your little game, I'm not sure she'd have been quite so faithful."

"Jean was fully onto the whole thing. She never tried to stop her brother. She wanted my ex out of the way. She wanted to help me get my daughter back from him. She only started cracking once Marci was there with the two of them alone. She'd also begged me on the telephone to go up there, to Fable. I told her I needed to stay put, until everything had died down, that the cops could suspect my involvement. Contacting you, detective has also helped me get full custody of my daughter. The private family court last week were impressed with my efforts to find her, and disappointed with the efforts made by the city cops. They decided I was a fit and loving mother, and I think that's beyond reproach. I would die for my baby."

I knew this was true. Anna had helped dispatch an evil man who had controlled her for years and taken her only child away from her. She'd used me, used people who cared about her, played a part in two deaths, and almost mine. But who was I to separate mother and daughter? As a private detective I didn't follow the law, my business was serving my clients. My world was one where justice was more than the electric chair, or a lifetime in the can. I asked if I could see Marci for one last time. Anna opened the door and the girl was curled up in bed, but still awake.

"Who's the man?" she asked.

"It's Mr Mitchell, the man who bought you back to mommy."

"Well, it was nice knowing you Miss Alessi," I said to the girl. "I hope good things come to you."

"We won't be using that name anymore detective," replied Anna, "From now on this is Marci Pierce. My maiden name."

"Pleased to meet you Miss Pierce, you be good to your mother now."

"She will, won't you dear?" said Anna, as she brushed her hand down the side of her daughter's face. "She's a good girl."

Before Anna let me out she took me in her arms.

"And thank you Brix for all you've done for us."

She planted her lips firmly on mine. I wasn't shy, and we kissed long and hard. It wasn't enough. But it was enough. The dame was dynamite, but I didn't want to be in any deeper. People who went in deeper usually didn't live too long. I left the apartment and walked into the night. There was a faint breeze wafting the scent of lilies around my nostrils. The sky was clear, and the distant stars, as old as time itself were shining down on the city. I made my way back to my car, through a row of palms, and I heard a rustle in the leaves just in time to see a big rat slinking down a trunk and running off towards the city, which made this hardened detective quiver.

My ride purred into life and I lit another Lucky.

Life and death, love and hate, sin and human desire are as permanent as the stars. There would always be guys like me looking for the truth, and saving a few souls in the process. And if I'd saved a heart of darkness that beat with a pure, unconditional love for her innocent child, then it had all been worth it.

I put my foot on the gas and went home.

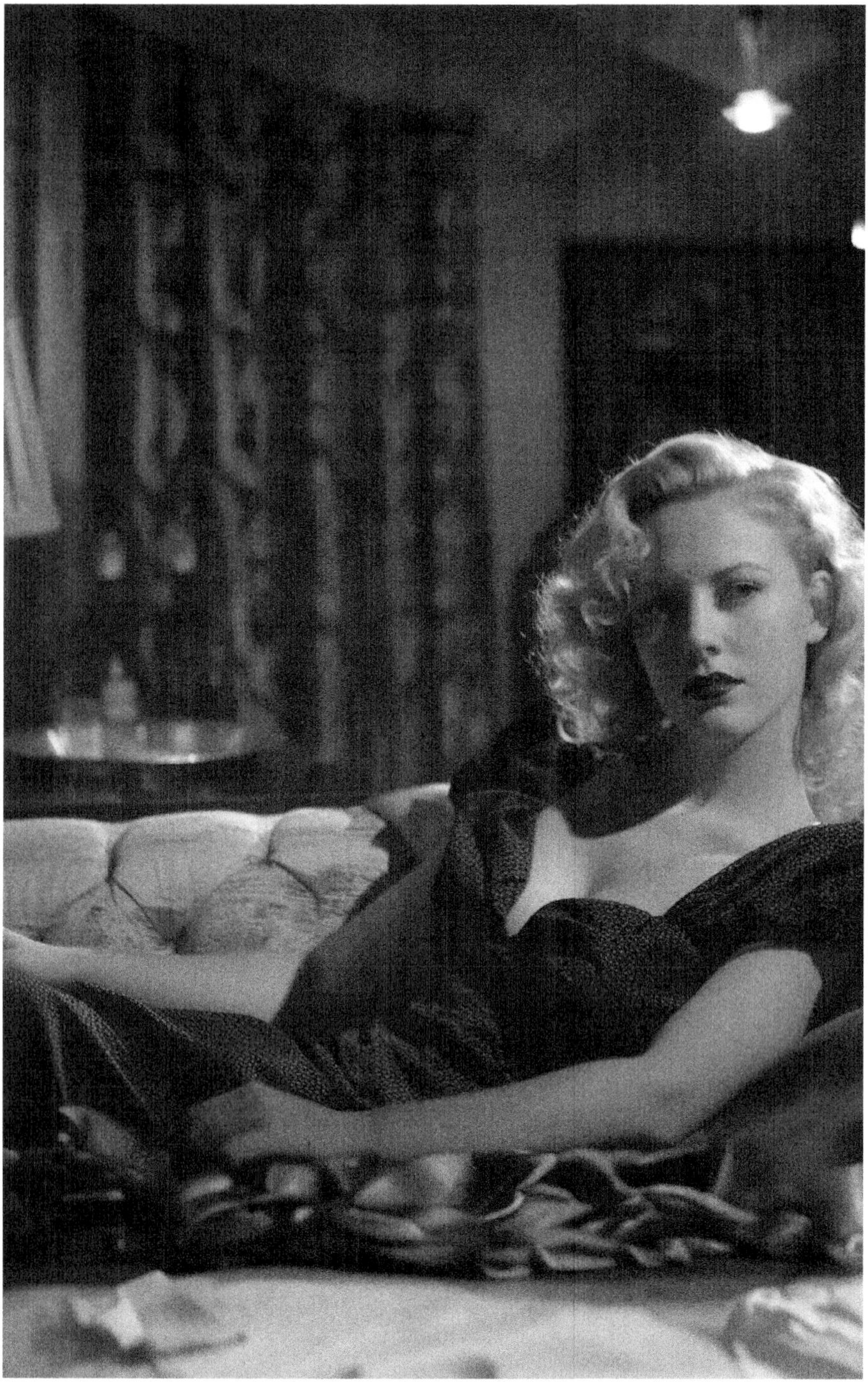

Thank You

There are a great many people I'd like to thank for their support, advice, and encouragement in getting this book published. If I've forgotten anyone below, please forgive me and know that you all have my thanks and gratitude.

I would like to thank all my social media friends who showed enthusiasm for the serialised "Facebook Status Novella" that became the book you are holding in your hands.

Special thanks for opinions and input to :

Diane Sprouse Hutchens (Femme Fatale), Molly Garcia, David St John (World Record Holder), Jennifer Ashcroft, Rebecca Guy, Gaz Marson and Ritchie Arrowsmith (The Man Who Knows Too Much).

And thanks for support and encouragement to:

Mihaela Benghea (The Dark Goddess), Margaret Harold, Debbie Clift, Holly Khan, Maddie Black, Mike Arias, Susan Freedman Varbero, Paul & Kiya Meadows, Nick Jordan, Stephanie Benyak, Damian Cullinane, Gill Forth, Jamie Cooper, Lee Kutt, Mandi Davies, Andy Parry, Andrea Collins, Ron E Hecht, Rod & Alicia, Jeanne Griffin, Jane Caroline Dass, Kevin England, Glenn O'Neill Kane, Peter Neithercott, David Aldridge, Judith Maunder, Tova Aviannah, Artemesia Dadarshi, Karen Ralls, Dazzy Connolley, Matthew "Marmaduke" Wright, Phil Archer, Jason Poynton, Greg Lubinsky, David Turner, Zoe Herdman, Nico Coleman, Rebecca Sarah Jane Reynolds, Surbhi Chauhan, Gabi Voicu, Darrell Terry, Jah Sky, Linsey Jo, Iain Grice, Richard Milton, Paul "Cap" Cooper, Jason Marsh, Jay Strongman, Elizabeth "Thorny" Rose, Lisa Edelman, Sun Tzu, Steve Potter, Bill Thompson, Greg Scorzo, Gail Paardekooper, Janet McCandles, Dom Geraghty, Steven Kruh, Sandy Penny, Kelle Grace Gaddis, Esther Bloom, Gordon Hopkinson, David Cohen, Damjana Finci, Maristella Sabino, Irinia Zvenigovo, Mark and Joseph Davis, Carina "Cici" Powell and family, Kevin Armstrong, Carol Newman, Sue Cole, Jessie Head, Amanda Dee, Karen "Kaz" Owen, Teeny Weena, Chris Butler, Angela Nicholls, Matthew Guy Sear, Ali Arellano, Dave Krynski, Chris DiBella, Paul Ingram, Claire

Alison, Ayn Riggs, Michelle Nicholls, Margaret and Steve Groves, Laura Maitland, Trebor Hash, Penny Black, Kathleen Myron, Dougie McGrath, Phil Simmons, Donna Renwick, Paula Bladon, Tony Gee, Jay Simon (actor), Caitlin Adams, Melissa Turnbull, Mark Flint, Adam Saunders, Richard Hanstock, Rebecca Warren, Tracy Fearndog, Helen Bradshaw-Tascon, Dominic Johnson, Martyn Hasbeen, Sarah Dekany, Lynn Trilby Gard, Marilyn Burgess, Paul J Sippits, Jac Parry, Gaynor Bond, Euphrosene Labon, Katie Carina Homer, Peter Murphy, Michael Johnson, Jane Pugh, Steve Simpson, Tabatha Caplan, Burl Ives, Michael Joey Taylor, Hannah Perks, Wendy Beardmore, Steven Marsh, Paul Bullock, Susan Henry, Adrian Morgan, Suzanne Sear, Lisa Dodd, Matthew Drury, Daniel Jupp, Dawn Taylor, Bex McLoughlin, Stacey Pearce Sargent, Veronica Heminsley, Karl Henry, Marie Dawkes, Lola Mencarini, Rose Jones, Mike Adlam, Kelsey Hancox, Jacqueline Laing, Debbie Gray, Michael Mellor, Susan Lynn Koerner, Shirley Robertson, Beverley Mason, Ilana Taub, Mike Worrall (artist), David Bush, Paul and Andrew Garner, Martin Jennings, Mark Ralls, David Ransford (Stig).

And you, the person reading this book, because after all, I write for you.